Vile Blood 2

Reflections

Dedication

To both the great mothers in my life; my mom who is also one of my best friends, and my mother-in-law who has given me so much strength and love over the years. I am blessed to have had both of you in my life!

Prologue

Let me tell you a story, it's about demons and how they came to be. From the moment there was sin there were demons. Some are born never knowing the light of day, already damned into darkness, but others had to earn their damnation. These were demons that were born human, and while some changed because of infected blood, there are a few who became demonic after becoming truly evil. Whether it was from selling their souls or just losing them, these people were void of humanity and evolved into something vile and sinister. And it was these depraved creatures that were the origins to demons; breeding new races throughout hundreds of generations.

Within time these beasts began to crave blood and flesh until it became a part of their DNA. Outcast by all gods, the demons grew to fear holy emblems; the ankh especially, since it was one of the oldest and most recognized symbols amongst these ancient creatures.

The blood of demons was a disease to humans; it was tainted with evilness, and would infect those who came into contact with it, bringing out the wickedness in their own souls. Some people turned fouler and faster than others, but a few could manage to preserve some semblance of humanity; but either way, to survive once becoming infected, the subject would have to continuously consume blood to keep their own stabilized. These half breed demons are vil sangs. They mostly walk in human form, but when enticed, their demonic features such as glowing eyes and fangs would emerge. Over time they could grow more demonic both in looks and in strength.

Vil sangs are on the bottom of the demonic pyramid; the weakest of their kind, they are usually looked down upon by full blooded demons. Vil sangs are commonly made by other vil sangs, since demons despised them; but a few are made by true demons, whether it is out of boredom or for a different form of torture.

The vil sang disease is one that cannot be cured; the demonic blood is too powerful and quickly works its way through the human body. There is no vaccination to prevent it, anyone who had blood-to-blood contact would surely become a vil sang.

With the birth of demons came warriors who would fight them, mortal men who trained and earned their strength. They would hunt and kill demons to cleanse humanity. Some of these warriors hunted in clans while others hunted alone, but all of which would devote their lives to the mission, giving up anything that would ensure their success. It usually led to a hard life, but none as cruel as that of a girl who was born and then thrown into an instant and constant struggle for survival.

Sarain knew nothing else.

Chapter 1

She could feel his eyes intensely on her; he had been watching her all night, waiting to get her alone. But that time wasn't yet to come, she wanted to dance, and knew the perfect place they could go.

She brought him to what appeared to be just an ordinary warehouse downtown. The outside had a large red X spray painted on the brick; it looked like simple graffiti. The man looked up at the building with a strange look, he thought that perhaps she was lost, but she assured him that this was the intended destination.

At the door they were greeted by a large stern man who gave the woman an once-over look before letting them both in. The man got the impression that the bouncer recognized the woman as a regular.

Inside was dark and only lit by surging colorful spotlights that flashed around the large room. Many people danced inside to an endless pulsating beat that blasted from speakers placed above in the rafters. Most people were dressed dark and looked very pale, but it was hard for the man to be sure in the poorly lit room.

The woman led him into the crowd like she fit right in even though she stood out in her bright red dress. She took him by the hand and he followed her out. Lights flashed as the woman moved seductively against the man. The music was fast but the woman danced slow, lingering close to him in a longing manner.

She leaned in towards him as if she were going to kiss him, but then pulled back at the last second just to tease him. He smiled at her, and when she did it again, he quickly moved in to get the kiss, but she was surprisingly too fast for him. Instead, he got a deep sniff of her hair and he thought of how good she smelled.

And as if reading his mind, she said, "I taste even better." She then leaned in and whispered into his ear, "Let's go somewhere more private."

She took him by the hand once more and led him to another door other than the exit.

"Where are we going?" he asked.

"You'll see soon enough," she said to him with a smile.

Behind the door was a staircase leading down into a dark corridor. The man found it odd, but didn't really care if it meant he could be alone with her. The stairs went a ways down, so much that the man could no longer hear the music from the club above. When they reached the bottom the woman pressed the man against a wall. She started to move in closer to him, her skin brushed up against his, she felt warm against his cool skin.

He looked at her lustfully and asked, "Are you ready to let me have that taste?"

She smiled and then suddenly yelled out, "Now!" And seemingly out of nowhere, two large men came out of the darkness.

The man quickly made a motion to move, but the woman knocked him back against the wall with incredible force. The man's eyes then lit up and his fangs and true self came out. He looked over at the two men and noticed that their faces were deformed like gargoyles and their skins were gray.

"What is this?" he shouted out, "She's the one who's human!"

They didn't listen and grabbed the vil sang man instead. He struggled as they dragged him deeper into the underground corridor, where he saw a large metal contraption standing in the middle of the room.

The woman walked over to it and flipped a switch causing the metal pieces to start moving, and the vil sang soon realized what it was; it was a giant meat grinder.

The vil sang continued to holler as the bigger beasts brought him closer to the grinder. Then he gave the woman one last look and muttered out, "You bitch," before the beasts threw him in.

She watched as the metal sliced through his flesh until his screaming stopped. She never closed, nor looked away with her violet eyes.

Sarain walked out of the dark club, feeling dirty for having let that vil sang man touch her; but she was glad to have finally gotten rid of a beast that had killed many naïve young women. She had been tracking him for some time after learning of many similar deaths of attractive young women, whose bodies were all found near clubs and all wearing red dresses; the man had a very particular taste in women, and tonight Sarain had fit that image.

Sarain had learned a new way to hunt, a way of letting the monsters come to her, and even a way of working with them. Three years had passed since the first time she had fought next to someone with demon blood in their veins, and now she saw the world differently. She was twenty-three and much wiser. Now she worked with the owners of an underground vil sang club called The X. The owners were demonic vil sangs who specialized in selling rare meats. Sarain had a deal with them, she would stay away from them and their regular customers if they wouldn't sell human. So far the deal was working well.

The actual club wasn't open to the public; vil sangs only. It was a place for them to mingle with their own kind and take sanctuary. Many of them practiced sustaining their urges, and only drank enough blood to feed and not to kill. Every now and then the club would allow a regular friendly human in, if it was a known sustaining partner to a vil sang, but never was a human allowed in unaccompanied without a vil sang. Only Sarain had that privilege, as part of her agreement with the owners. And she would occasionally bring them demons to dispose of as meat; it kept her from having to worry about clean up and carcasses left behind to be found by unknowing people.

The night air was cool with a light breeze. Sarain felt her long dark hair flutter behind her. She walked down the dark alley away from the club when a police car quickly pulled up to her and came to a sudden stop. Its lights were flashing but the siren was off. She held her dress down from the gust of wind, and stared curiously at the cop car. The driver's door then opened, and a tall strong looking man stepped out with a stern look on his face. He had a shiny badge pinned to his uniform. This first caught Sarain's attention, next was the gun in his holster.

He looked over at her and muttered out, "This isn't a place a little lady like you should be. It's not safe."

"I think I can handle it," Sarain responded back.

"I wouldn't be too sure about that," he said as he began to approach her.

Was he serious? She thought to herself with almost a chuckle in her head.

The man continued to approach Sarain, and when he finally stood right in front of her, he stopped and glared down at her. She knew he had no probable cause to stop her, but still he stood blocking her way. Sarain could feel the tension pulsating off of him, and when he made a motion to move she quickly reacted by grabbing him by his shirt.

"I can get you for assaulting a police officer," he stated, but she ignored him.

Instead Sarain tugged at his shirt and pulled him down to her eye level. The man had a look of surprise in his eyes, caught off guard by her strength. He waited for her to make her move, but Sarain's expression softened and she smiled at the officer then she leaned in and kissed him hungrily.

He placed his arms around her and kissed her back with just as much passion.

This officer was no stranger to Sarain, she had known him for nearly two years, and they had been a couple for most of that time. His name was Eddie, though she called him by his given name, Edward, even though he didn't prefer it, but he let only her get away with it.

They had met one night when Eddie was responding to a call about screams coming from an abandoned building downtown. It was a known den for crack-heads and homeless people, so Eddie figured it was going to be a routine sweep; he and his partner had shoed people out of there before with little hassle. But this time when he walked into the crumbling building, he immediately saw blood all over the walls. And when he and his partner discovered the partially eaten body of a homeless man, Eddie went and called for backup.

They had thought the place was secure enough, but while Eddie was on the radio he heard his partner let out a blood curdling scream. Eddie ran back inside to find a scaly creature on top of his partner, and mauling at his throat.

Eddie took out his gun and began shooting the beast, but it didn't seem to faze it. The creature lunged at Eddie, but midway through the air something else flew at the beast. It was Sarain. She was on the monster before Eddie was even aware of anyone else being there. And it was in moments that she had the beast down and decapitated.

Eddie was stunned at first, but then asked Sarain what had just happened. All she responded was, "A demon happened." Then she left without further explanation.

After that, Eddie came across Sarain more and more while on the job. Each time she told him a little more, until finally she sat down with him and explained about demons: how they worked and how to kill them. It was after that, that Eddie began helping her, whether it was fighting by her side or just covering up after her kills. And one day after a particularly long night of hunting, Sarain turned her attention on to Eddie, and began kissing him without a word. It was from then on that any time they saw each other things usually took a passionate turn.

Tonight was no different, and after a few hours at Eddie's place Sarain found herself dressing and slipping out while he slept. She was always invited to stay, but never did. She wasn't comfortable sleeping next to someone, always worrying that her constant nightmares would open up too many questions she wasn't prepared to answer. She figured the less Eddie knew about her the better, and besides she didn't want to get too attached; she was always on the move, and might one day have to leave him behind.

She was prepared to do so.

Chapter 2

A knock at the door jarred Sarain out of sleep. It had already become night, but she still felt tired from her vigorous night before. Nevertheless, Sarain was glad to get up; she had been dreaming about him again; memories from her past that she didn't want to look back on. She quickly dressed with the knocks still coming from her door before finally she was ready to answer it.

A man stood on the other side, or at least he looked like a man; Sarain knew better though, this wasn't a man, he was a vil sang, and she had grown able to tell the distinction in an instant. He looked panicked and desperate; he had to be to come to her door. Sarain knew that the man wouldn't be able to step inside, he couldn't cross the barrier she had hidden in the door frame. It was a barrier to keep out evil beings that she was now cleverly hiding in the frames and sills of her home; better to not alert people to her strange behavior and the barriers didn't need to be constantly redone.

Sarain looked at the man and said, "You have a lot of nerve coming here, you know what I do to your kind."

"I do, but I heard you also know the difference between creatures that are evil and ones that aren't," he replied distraughtly.

Sarain looked into the vil sang's helpless eyes and could see that he meant her no harm. She could tell the difference, it was something she looked for now, before she would kill any vil sangs; whether or not they were actually evil and not just genetically so. Sarain had learned a lot in the three years since defeating Sephor.

"What do you want?" Sarain finally asked.

"I need your help, and I heard that you're experienced in these kinds of situations," he answered.

"I don't really help your kind," Sarain quickly stated.

"But it's my children that need your help," he frantically said, "They're my children from when I was human, and they still are. A vil sang couple has them and plans to kill them."

"Okay," she responded and then asked, "Why can't you get them on your own?"

"They aren't regular vil sangs, they're more… more…" he trailed off thinking of a word to describe them.

Sarain finally stopped him by saying, "Demonic?"

"Yes," he replied, "And they are too strong for me to take on alone."

This could have been a trap, but Sarain was still curious. She continued to talk to him and learned that the man's name was James, and that both his son and daughter had been taken by this demonic vil sang couple. It was the same couple that had turned him only a few of years earlier. They were not pleased with his progression as a vil sang, and felt that his children were too strong of a tie to his humanity, and needed to be disposed of. James wasn't willing to lose his children, and knew that if they were to be saved something would have to be done fast. That's why he had come to Sarain. She had been in this particular town for nearly two years and had made quite a name for herself on the streets there. He had learned that if anyone could save his children it would be Sarain.

Sarain never could turn her back on children, if there really was a chance to save a child she had to take it. She got more information on the vil sang couple such as their whereabouts and interests. Their names were Cyrus and Desmina, and they had been together for more than three hundred years. Cyrus had a weakness for beautiful women and Desmina had a weakness for Cyrus, she was completely devoted to him.

Sarain accepted the mission; demonic vil sangs seemed to be popping up more frequently, and were getting to be easy to take care, especially now that she had a few tricks up her sleeve, and someone to back her up.

Sarain and Eddie waited outside a bar for the last member of their new trio to arrive. Eddie continuously looked at his watch, checking the time until he finally said, "He's late. Why do we even have to wait for this guy? It'll be fine just the two of us."

Sarain sighed and explained, "You've never dealt with a demonic vil sang, they are much stronger than your everyday ones. Besides, it's his children we are trying to save; he has a right to be there, Edward."

"Well I'm not waiting here much longer," he protested.

"Yes, you are," Sarain stated, it came out like an order, but then she reached over and caressed Eddie's cheek, and added, "Because you'll do it for me."

Eddie's expression softened and he gave her a smirk. He took a hold of her hand and kissed it, then he told her, "You know I can't say 'no' to you." He then leaned in to kiss her, but Sarain pulled back and motioned to someone who was approaching. Eddie looked over to see a man who appeared to be in his thirties with dirty blond hair and pale skin walking towards them. The man looked like a jock and was prettier than Eddie's liking; he didn't like the idea of such a man visiting Sarain's home, vil sang or not.

The man stopped in front of Sarain and gave her a look of recognition, then turned to Eddie and gave him a once over. Catching his questioning gaze, Sarain noted, "James, this is Edward, he'll be joining us."

"It's Eddie," Eddie quickly added. James gave him a glance, but said nothing in response, as if not interested; instead he turned to Sarain and asked, "Are you ready for me to take you to their lair?"

"Yes, a full-on attack without them suspecting would be best. If they were to find out you recruited backup beforehand, it might give them time to prepare an attack back, or it could scare them into getting rid of the weight that is your children," Sarain speculated.

"I can't have that," James stated.

"I know, that's why we're moving in fast," she replied.

They followed James, all on foot, down different alleys and narrow walk ways. A car would be too noisy and can easily be heard coming. The lair was supposedly two miles away from their start point, but all the twists and turns down alleyways made the trip seem longer. The sky was black except for the bright nearly full moon. The streets were wet from an earlier rain and the moon reflected its light in the puddles on the ground. As they neared their destination, James put his hand out to signal them to slow their pace, and they crept the rest of the way. He then pointed down to a dingy short stairway leading to a basement floor apartment. The building looked old and decrepit, it appeared abandoned, and Sarain doubted that the building still had paying tenants. It looked like a perfect place for a vil sang to hole up in.

James went down first, he gave the door knob a quick shake, but the door was stuck on something, perhaps its frame had swelled from the humid air. It didn't matter either way, he planned on getting in. James kicked the door in, and this signaled Sarain and Eddie to hurry down the stairs. They had to move quickly now, since their entrance was likely to have been heard. They rushed into the dark building, weapons in hand. Eddie making sure to keep a close and watchful eye on Sarain, even though she was much stronger and skilled as a fighter than him, he still felt protective of her. James continued to lead the way. Inside the building was water damaged, tumbled over broken down furniture, holes in the walls, rodents, and insects. Mold was growing on the walls and floors, and the air had a sour pungent stench to it. It wasn't a place that a human, even a vagrant, would choose to stay in. The place was silent, and the three of them began to search the building from room to room. Sarain had initially thought that the place was a mere apartment building, but in fact the place was more like a large condo-like house. Each room they checked stood empty of both people and of décor. It didn't look like anyone had been living there, but James assured them they were in the right place. They then went down a long narrow hallway, and as they walked, the stench grew thicker. James still led the way, but Sarain was beginning to feel like him leading was a bad idea; she knew what that smell was, and the silence only further backed her suspicions.

James turned the corner then quickly came to an abrupt stop. His blade dropped from his hand and splashed in a puddle on the floor. Eddie noticed the puddle was dark and looked thick then he too realized what Sarain had already foreseen. The floor was covered in blood, blood also stained the walls, and inside the room, just around the corner from Sarain and Eddie laid the decaying bodies of two young children; James' children.

James dropped to his knees, but when Sarain saw the blood rapidly soaking into his clothes, she quickly grabbed him by the arm and yanked him up. Eddie then reached for James' blade, but Sarain called out, "Leave it!" She didn't want James to be handed a blade covered in his kids' blood.

It was obvious due to the decay that James' children had been killed soon after they were abducted. They were likely dead long before James had even come to Sarain for help, there was nothing she could have done to stop it. Still, Sarain felt at fault, like their deaths were somehow tied to her, it was a feeling she always got when she found children the victims of demonic attacks, ever since she lost Kit. She glanced quickly then turned away from the sight of the two small tattered bodies. She closed her eyes and the image of Kit lying limp and cold in an empty dark room flashed into her mind. She felt a tear escape her eye, but quickly wiped it away, she didn't like to show her emotions.

Eddie was watching Sarain through the corner of his eye and noticed her try to hide the fact that she was crying. Eddie had never seen Sarain cry before, and was surprised that she would bother to hide her emotions at a time like this and even with James himself crying while standing only a foot away. It bothered Eddie that Sarain kept up with her hard exterior, her purposely hiding her feelings seemed worse to him than if she had remained emotionless. Eddie didn't know how to make her open up, he knew this wasn't the time, but he wasn't sure if he would ever see a lighter side of Sarain.

Sarain stepped forward, and took a quick look around. Aside from the corpses, the place was empty of people. She shook her head, and said, "It looks like they left this place days ago, they could be anywhere by now."

"But my kids… my kids…" James stammered.

"Your kids are gone! There's nothing we can do!" Sarain shouted at him, hoping he would shut up.

"We could bury them," Eddie muttered. Sarain turned and shot him a look then stated, "Because carrying around a couple of dead bodies sounds like a good idea. We have to leave them." She was annoyed that Eddie could make such an obvious mistake; she didn't understand that he was trying to be sympathetic to James.

"We need to search the place for anything that might be a clue to where they could have gone," Sarain ordered, "Edward, you and James take the other rooms." This was her way of being supportive to James, not having him search the room where his kids' bodies laid.

Eddie nodded to her, and led James out of the room. Sarain then started searching around. As she searched through the ghastly room the pungent smell seemed to grow stronger and was enough to make anyone gag, but it was a part of the life Sarain was used to. It was looking hopeless when something suddenly caught Sarain's eyes, a black mirror hanging on the wall. Sarain did a double take when she saw it; something seemed odd to her about the mirror, mostly because it showed her reflection, and nothing else. Never had she looked in a mirror and only seen her own reflection. She approached it cautiously, and studied the mirror more closely. It had a metal frame which had what looked to be hand carved details. The metal was tarnished and the mirror looked very old. Sarain watched both herself and her surroundings in its reflection, all appeared normal, and nothing was out of place. The fact that the mirror seemed ordinary was what made it feel so special to Sarain, like it could give her the peace that no other mirror could.

Soon both James and Eddie came walking back down the hall, Eddie was carrying a big dusty old book in his hands, while James was empty handed.

"This is all we found," Eddie said while holding up the book, "It was buried under some debris. It appears to be a handwritten journal, but I'm not sure of what, some of the entries look kind of strange. I thought you might want to take a look."

"We'll take it with us," Sarain said, and she turned and looked back at the mirror. She then reached up and took it off the wall, "We're taking this too."

Eddie looked at her with confusion, but didn't question her. They followed her out, James hanging his head down and keeping his eyes low. Sarain never offered any words of condolence, so Eddie in her stead asked him, "Are you alright?"

"My children are dead, do you think I'm alright?" James replied with a tone.

Sarain glanced over at James and finally said, "We'll find the creatures that did it. Your children won't go un-avenged."

"Maybe so, either way, when I find them I will tear into them with every ounce of strength I have, just as they did to my children," he muttered in response.

Sarain lowered her eyes, she hoped that James would have his revenge, but she knew from experience that getting revenge never took away the pain nor lessened it. Nothing would fill that void, and something so heart-wrenching could not be forgotten. She knew James could never have children again, damned humans could not reproduce.

Normally she didn't care about the welfare of any vil sangs, but something about James' situation dug at her; parents sometimes lose their children, but never do they have an eternity to mourn them.

Chapter 3

There was nothing really either Sarain or Eddie could do, so they left James alone. He went his separate way, and they weren't sure if they would ever see him again. Sarain wouldn't give up looking for the demonic vil sangs that killed his children, but she didn't think it was likely that they would find them. Both she and Eddie walked in silence; he could tell something was bothering her. They had lost innocents before, but it was always a different feeling to lose children. It was only then that Sarain ever appeared affected by the casualties. Eddie wanted to discuss it with her, but the look on her face told him not to press the subject.

Eddie walked Sarain home where he left her to be alone; she always sought solitude after a bad night. She placed the old book on her desk, and walked to her closet. Inside it she shuffled around until she reemerged with a photo in her hand. The photo was of a woman in her early twenties with long dark hair and vibrant brown eyes. She had a sweet smile, but a somewhat sorrowful look on her face, and inside her arms she clutched a small child. It was a curly haired girl who looked scared and was trying to hide her eyes. It had been the girl's first photo, and she had been frightened of the camera. Sarain remembered well, because she was the girl, and the woman was her mother, Ariana. Sarain had always wondered what her mother had been thinking of when the picture was taken, whatever it was seemed to make her sad.

Sarain had few memories of her mother; she died when Sarain was only five. Her mother had been twenty-three, the same age Sarain was now. Sarain thought of how short her mother's life had been, and wondered how her life would have been different if her mother had lived. But then she also had those same thoughts about her clan. Sarain put down the picture, and then picked up the mirror she had taken from the dank lair. She looked into it and saw her face staring back. Her violet eyes looked tired, and she realized her skin was beginning to get pale. She hardly ever went out during daylight hours anymore; her prey was nocturnal, and so was she.

Sarain took the mirror, and hung it up on the wall. She wasn't one for decorating, but the mirror fascinated her. She wondered what made it not show her the visions that were constantly haunting her. She then turned back to her desk and gazed over at the journal that Eddie had found. It looked old, and was partly damaged from water. Sarain picked it up and began to flip through its pages. Some of the writing had bled and become incomprehensible, and some of the pages were stuck together and were too frail to pry apart.

She tried to make sense of what the book was about, but its notes seemed random. Then she saw an entry that was familiar to her; it was the recipe for a barrier spell. All the ingredients were there along with a few new ones that further helped keep out evil beings.

Sarain looked in amazement. She flipped a couple of pages and found precise descriptions on how to kill demons of different types and origins. It described spots to hit to break through the hard scaly hides of stronger demons. Sarain scanned and skimmed through more pages, and realized that she was looking at a hunter's handbook. She had never seen such a thing before, and was surprised that it had been found in a demon's lair. Then she realized that the demons must have taken it from a hunter they had likely killed.

A wave of sadness hit Sarain; someone's life work had gone into this book, and it had become a demon's garbage. But now she had it to care for, and could add on to it. She marveled at the possibilities of what knowledge this book might hold, and what it could teach her. She flipped further into the book and noticed a peculiar entry. It was titled "Ancients". In it, it told of a legend about a rare breed of mythical demons, ones without weaknesses or any semblance of a soul. The writer also often referred to them as "The Damned", and stated that these creatures were once humans cast into damnation without the help of tainted blood. They were described as the worst of mankind, and were so evil that they lost their souls.

Sarain noticed that the author failed to give a description of these beasts, but believed that it was probably because no one had ever seen one or at least lived to talk about it. She had learned from experience that the more evil a demon was, the more demonically deformed it became. She imagined that one of these Ancients, if they existed, would have to be the most frightening thing that could ever be imagined, if it was even possible to be imagined.

She continued to read on and learned that the author had heard rumors that a real Ancient was alive and living in a small primitive town set in a rural countryside. The writer went on to say how he tracked down the supposed town and did find a large array of beasts but none so great in which could be one of these Ancients. The hunter then investigated several other possible cases of an Ancient, but most panned out to be bogus. All except one, it was a case in which an entire village of trained hunters was wiped out overnight. It was said that when the village was found by a small party of hunters who often affiliated with these villagers, they found that the village's barriers were left untouched, but all the occupants inside were brutally murdered and their bodies desecrated.

Sarain's heart began to pound, it sounded all too familiar; could the author be talking about her clan? She skimmed through the passage, but found nothing else of relevance to her people. She wondered if the author had believed that the villagers were all killed by one creature; she knew from memory that her clan had been destroyed by an army of beasts. Perhaps it was instances like this that people often contributed to the workings of these supposed Ancients.

But then a sick feeling hit the pit of Sarain's stomach; Sephor had told her that he hadn't been the one leading the attack on her clan, but that there had been someone higher up than he. She had hoped that he had been lying to her, as some final way of screwing with her mind. But she had never found an explanation as to how her clan's barriers could be breached, but not actually broken. And apparently the author of this handbook couldn't find one either.

"The barriers were left untouched," the phrase kept spinning through Sarain's head, "The barriers were left untouched." How could that be? If there was someone else left responsible for the death of her clan, even if it was some kind of legendary demon, she had to find it, track it down, and kill it.

The entry ended, and the author went on about something new. He talked about mixtures of the right kinds of metal ores to make stronger blades that wouldn't break so easily on the harder demons' hides, but the subject was of no interest to Sarain. She wanted to learn more about Ancients, and if they could possibly exist. But she knew in her heart that if she wanted to find out more, she would have to do it herself. She just didn't know where to start.

A few days had gone by since that night; all the while Sarain had been studying from her newly acquired handbook and hunting as routine. Tonight she hunted with Eddie by her side, it was something they often did when Eddie could find the time from work; his nights were usually busy working as a cop. He wasn't as experienced as Sarain, nor was his skills as honed, but his presence was still helpful, and he often kept monsters off Sarain's back whenever they found multiple demons together.

Sarain had never trained a hunter before, and rarely ever came across one, but she found Eddie's eagerness to learn appealing. And in the time that she has known him, his ability to keep up had improved dramatically. Still, she didn't want him hunting alone, and even though she was quite capable, she had the feeling that he didn't want her hunting alone as well.

The night air was muggy, humid from another early rain, and the ground was still damp all around. It would be harder to find creatures on a night like this since most people didn't like to be out in such weather, which gave the beasts less targets to find. But sometimes this also came as an advantage: if a demon was hungry enough, it might be willing to come out of hiding, and even brave enough to attack a hunter.

The now full moon was mostly covered by heavy rain clouds that lingered until they would be ready to release another bout of rain. The clouds made the night darker than Sarain had expected, every turn had been filled with more shadows, and every dark crevasse had been harder to explore. Eddie in particular was having a hard time seeing that night, and had nearly tripped on a number of cluttering objects on the ground, so much so that Sarain was beginning to get annoyed. Yes, it was indeed darker, but she was still able to see, and in her mind, Eddie should be able to as well.

They had trekked for many hours of the night with no signs of a beast. Eddie was starting to slow down, and appeared a bit winded until he finally stopped and said while breathing heavily, "I need a break, this humidity is killing me."

"Every minute we waste is an opportunity we lose. If we're not the ones to find these beasts, then that means they're finding innocent victims," Sarain spoke sternly.

"I know, I know," Eddie panted, and continued, "But I'm of no use exhausted."

"Then perhaps you should go home," she stated.

He stared at her for a moment and then said, "I don't want to fight with you. You know I don't like you hunting without me, and you know I'm not leaving, so there's really no point in arguing with me. I'm not going anywhere."

She turned around to look at him, but suddenly yelled out, "Down!"

Eddie reacted fast and dropped to the ground just in time to have a demon fly over his head. It just barely missed him, and landed on the ground in between them. Sarain charged at the creature with her blade ready. She swung and it quickly raised its arm to block her, but the beast underestimated her strength, because her blade sliced halfway through its arm, through its rough exterior, until it hit the bone. The demon roared in pain and swatted at Sarain who jumped back, missing its attack. It tried to charge her, but was stopped when it was surprised from behind by Eddie. It must have forgotten him, or didn't see him as a threat, because it was caught off guard when Eddie moved his blade around its neck and in front of its throat. Then with both hands on the blade, he thrust back the weapon until he sawed through the bone. Its head dropped to the ground before its body crumpled.

Black blood oozed from its neck, and most of the spray went outward away from Eddie.

He looked over at Sarain who had a look of relief on her face. Tired or not, Eddie still had good reflexes, and Sarain was thankful for that. Eddie moved back from the carcass and lowered his blade. Sarain soon rushed to his side, she cupped the side of his face with one of her hands and stretched up to kiss him. She never should have doubted his capability.

That was the only demon they found that night, they made their way home a few hours later. Sarain followed Eddie back to his place. As he cleaned off their blades, Sarain looked at a picture of his parents framed by his bed, he had lost them both in a car accident a couple years before he met her, but he was always talking about them. They sounded like good people.

Eddie stepped into the room and noticed her admiring the photo. "How come you never talk about your parents?" he asked her.

Sarain set the picture back down, turned to him, and said, "There's not much to tell. My mother died when I was really young, and I never knew my father."

"Who raised you?" Eddie questioned with curiosity. He could never get Sarain to open up about her past, and was surprised now how willing she was to talk.

"My grandfather, but only until I was thirteen," she answered.

"Why's that?" he quickly inquired.

"Because he was murdered," she bluntly responded then added, "After that it was just me."

"Wait, how did you manage that? Didn't you have to go into foster care or something?" he asked confused.

"No, I lived on the streets and in abandoned property up until I was old enough to earn money," Sarain described, "Then I'd work odd jobs to make me enough money to get by for however long I'd plan to stay in that particular place."

"How much longer do you plan to stay in town here?" Eddie asked with a worried tone.

"Well, there's still a steady amount of aggressive creatures here. It's a regular hot spot. I won't leave until the number is cut down significantly," Sarain stated, catching Eddie's concern.

He walked over to her, put his arms around her, and gave her forehead a quick kiss. "It must have been hard for you growing up all alone. But you have me now, you never have to be alone again," he told her. His words were meant to make her feel happy, but instead Sarain was feeling a bit smothered, she didn't know how to tell him that once her task was done she didn't plan on staying. Eddie wasn't really at fault for it; Sarain just didn't know how to depend on someone. She did care for him, and she had let him get closer than anyone had ever been to her since she was a kid. But still it felt like something was lacking in her, like she was missing the ability to form a real attachment. Perhaps she was just blocking it herself; after all, she had lost so many people that it had made it harder for her to make a connection.

Sarain watched as Eddie took off his dirty shirt to clean up. She stared at him thinking how even though she still felt as though her guard was up, there was something about him that kept her wanting him around. Eddie glanced up and noticed her watchful eyes. Sarain walked over to him without a word and ran her hand over his short, cropped hair; its bristles lightly scratching the palm of her hand. His dark eyes stared down at her as she ran her hand over the skin of his cheek. She then moved her hand down his neck and he quickly grabbed a hold of her hand. He pulled her to him and leaned down to give her a tender kiss. His lips were soft, they were always soft, and his kiss always left her wanting more.

Eddie ran his hands through Sarain's long hair and down her back. He brought her closer to him till she was pressed against him, skin against skin. She took in his smell with a deep breath; he smelled salty, sweaty from the hot night, but she loved his scent, it reminded her of strength and safety. He kissed her again, this time with more hunger and passion. She placed her hands on his chest, and pressed on him as if to keep some distance between them, and did this even when they became one, until finally she gave in and embraced him fully.

Eddie kissed Sarain's cool skin with his warm lips, and worked his way up her neck and to her ear. Then he whispered to her, "When will you let me in?"

"You are in," she whispered back.

He moved his head back and looked her in the eyes, "No, in here," he said placing his hand over her heart. He had noticed after all. She stared at him for a moment then took his hand and held it in hers, their fingers interlocking. And with her other arm she wrapped it around his back and pulled him to her. She kissed him longingly, and wished to herself that she could give him what he needed from her. But she could only show him; the words weren't there, and she wasn't sure if they'd ever be.

Chapter 4

Once again Sarain waited till Eddie had fallen asleep before dressing, she still wasn't ready to stay the entire night with him. She slipped on her clothes then leaned down, kissed him on his head before leaving, and whispered, "Goodnight." He was sound asleep and never heard her leave. He had asked once before why she never stayed, but he had learned by now to stop asking.

Sarain went to her own home where she crawled into bed and fell fast asleep. All the talk of family must have lingered in the back of her mind, because Sarain found herself dreaming about her mother.

Little Sarain waited for her grandfather to leave her mother's room. She had been told to keep out, but she missed her mother and wanted to see her badly. She quietly played near the door till Delmar finally emerged, and upon exiting the room he gave Sarain a stern look and said in a strong voice, "You better not be planning on disturbing your mother. She needs her rest, so I better not catch you in there, because children who disobey get whipped."

Sarain stared up at her grandfather for a moment with wide eyes, but then went back to playing with her doll, as if the thought of defying him never had even crossed her mind. Delmar gave her another glance, and Sarain could feel his eyes watching her as she played, not trusting the young child's motives, but he eventually lost interest and left the child to her doll.

Sarain played for a minute longer, still suspecting that her grandfather might return, but when he didn't, she quickly put down her doll, and snuck to her mother's door. She cracked the door open and listened quietly outside it. It was silent, perhaps her mother was sleeping, but Sarain still wanted to see her. She cracked the door open a little more and quickly slipped inside. Sarain then slowly tip-toed to her mother's bed, her mother's eyes were closed and she appeared to be asleep.

Sarain stared at her mother who nearly looked like a stranger to her now, not only had it been a while since she had last seen her, but her usually tanned skin had grown pale, and her body had become frail. Her mother's beautiful long dark hair had lost its luster and was now matted beneath her and drenched in sweat. Sarain didn't like it, she wanted her old mom back; the one that used to sing and play with her. She wished she could fix her mother like the many times Ariana had fixed her daughter's pain, but wasn't sure how to.

The little girl moved closer to her mother, and put her hands up until they touched her mother's skin. Her mom felt cold, but Sarain held her hands in place regardless, she wanted to help her mother. She closed her eyes and thought about healing, and what she had seen her mother do. She tried to focus her thoughts, but her mind felt blurry. She continued to try, but nothing was happening. Then a sudden brush through her hair caused Sarain to quickly open her eyes. Ariana laid there looking down at her with a weak smile on her face. She had brushed her hand through her daughter's hair, and stared at her with her light brown eyes, that still hadn't quite lost their sparkle.

"It's okay if you can't do it, I never taught you how," Ariana spoke softly. Even still, Sarain gave her mother a sad look as though she had failed. Ariana caressed her child's face and said, "Don't be sad, my love. Some things can't be fixed, but it will never change how much I love you."

"But grandfather said that you might leave, and I don't want you to go, mommy," Sarain whimpered.

"We all have to leave some time, baby, but I will still always be by your side, even if you can't see me," Ariana sweetly told her crying daughter. She reached over and took a hold of Sarain's hand, and then said, "I wish I could've helped you more with the woman you will become, and the great things you will do someday."

She stared down at her daughter, but her eyes looked at her as though she was seeing something else other than the small child by her side. She took a deep breath and spoke to her, "You're going to have to be strong," she then got quiet for a moment, as if losing her train of thought, and then added, "He's going to need you." And the room grew silent again.

Sarain looked up at her mother with a tear in her eye, but saw that her mother was still gently breathing; she must have fallen back asleep. She wanted to wake her mother and ask her who it was who needed her; was it her grandfather? But she couldn't bring herself to disturb her mother again. She would let her rest. Sarain stretched up and gave her mother a kiss on her cheek, and then turned and walked towards the door. She gave her mother one last look before closing the door behind her. Perhaps if she had known that that would be the last time she would see her mother alive, she would have stayed longer, or woken her mother so that they could have finished their conversation. But instead Sarain went back to playing with her doll just outside Ariana's bedroom, never knowing what her mother meant by her last words.

Sarain was sleeping peacefully, so much so that she didn't sense an assault coming. She suddenly shot up in bed, she was being attacked, but as she searched the shadowy room with her eyes, she found no culprit in sight. Dawn was just barely approaching, but enough light was trickling in for Sarain to know that demons wouldn't be out. Then she was suddenly hit with another wave of pain, and realized that the attack was coming from inside. Throbbing pain shot throughout her body, and she felt like she was on fire. She had only experienced a similar feeling a few times in her life, one of those times being when she had found the strength to kill Sephor. But unlike that instance, Sarain had not been pushed to the brink, she wasn't being fueled by pure hatred, she was just living her everyday life. Still the hurting continued; stinging and aching shooting all over her body. Her muscles began to twitch, and her arms and legs started to shake. Sarain ignored this symptom; she was too focused on the pain pulsating in her skull. Her eyes burned especially, they felt like they were going to explode out of her head. Her hands went to her temples, and she rubbed them hoping to make the pain subside, but it didn't.

Finally Sarain could stand it no longer; she yelled out, "What the hell is going on?"

She clutched her fists tightly and slammed them on the bed; they bounced back up lightly as they hit the mattress. She realized that a sudden urge to do violence was building up inside her, she wanted to do what she could to make the pain stop, whatever it would take. She clutched her fists even tighter, and wished that it was night so that she could hunt down and wail on some kind of evil beast. She needed to beat the pain out of her body. The throbbing slowly began to lessen in her head, and disappear from her body until only her hands hurt. She unclenched her fists and opened her hands, then realized her palms felt sticky. Sarain looked down at her hands and noticed that they were bleeding; she had dug her nails into her palms until they bled. Droplets of crimson stained her bed sheet, just a few had fallen, but they stood out strongly on the silky white sheet.

Sarain wondered what had just happened, had she had some kind of seizure? She had never been a sickly person, and always healed quickly from injuries, but now she feared that there was something inside her that she couldn't battle away; something more deadly than a demon.

Her body still felt weak and tired, so she rested her head back down on her pillow. Her eyelids felt heavy, and she began to close them again. Suddenly something caught her attention over on the other side of the room, something was out of place. The black mirror she had recently added to the wall was reflecting an image that should not have been there; a face shown back watching over the room. It was unlike any vision she had ever seen before; normally memories played out in mirrors, but this was different. In the reflection, a familiar face stared out, and it was not like any memory she had. Delmar's eyes stared out, watching her from inside the mirror.

"Grandfather?" Sarain faintly whispered, but no reply came. She felt too weak to get up, and when she tried the room began to spin. Sarain collapsed back down on the bed, her vision blurred, and then it went black.

Sarain opened her eyes to a bright room, the midday sun was shining in. Her mind was hazy, and it took her a moment to realize what had happened a few hours earlier, the dried droplets of blood on her sheets helped refresh her memory. She glanced at her hands to see that the wounds from her nails had already healed, there was barely even a scratch left behind. Then the image her grandfather's face watching her from the mirror flashed into her mind.

She groaned as she got up to investigate the mirror, but from a distance, it appeared normal. Upon further inspection Sarain still found nothing wrong, the mirror still showed only her, a feat that was already strange for her, but nothing else special could be found. It was just a dark reflection of what was around, showing in the black mirror.

Sarain shook her head, she had seen weird things in mirrors before; memories mostly, usually in which she saw the dead, but never like this; never with them watching back at her. She decided she must have been dreaming, or her mind could have been playing tricks on her after a long strenuous night. That migraine she had had surely didn't help, and it was something she should be more worried about, that headache came from out of nowhere. She had never experienced such a pain before. Besides, if Sarain was capable of seeing the dead, there was one person in particular she would want to see, and it wasn't her grandfather.

Sarain walked to her closet and slid back the door. A row of dark clothing hung, and she pushed them aside, behind them was a small black safe, and in that safe were the few remaining things she kept from her past. Most things she had long since left behind, others she had lost in the fire the night Kit was taken from her. But these were the few things she had left that she held dear. Sarain opened the safe and knew immediately what she was looking for; it was at the back of the safe pressed flat against it, carefully hidden from prying eyes, even though only she knew the combo to her safe. She pulled out the stiff piece of paper to expose an old photograph from her childhood. The photo had faded over time and its edges had become a little tattered, but in the picture still remained two smiling children. One was thirteen and the other was sixteen. The elder was a tall dark haired boy with hazel eyes, who went by the name Orran. The younger was Sarain whose black hair looked messy, and her violet eyes in the photo almost looked like a glare from the camera. To her the child version of herself looked awkward, but nevertheless the young Orran had an arm around her and posed happily with her in the picture, which was taken just a few weeks before the attack on her clan.

Sarain raised a finger to the picture and traced the image of Orran with it. He had been her dearest friend, and his death still remained the biggest heartbreak for her. She felt partly at fault for it, thinking if she hadn't broken his concentration or if she had come out of her hiding spot and to his aide, that perhaps together they could have gotten away, and then maybe Sarain wouldn't have had to grow up alone. She would give anything to be able to go back and change things.

Sarain gave the photo one last look before putting it back in its place, hidden in the safe. She thought to herself how she wished that mirrors would for once show her a happy memory rather than the gruesome ones it did. Her happy memories were few, and the gruesome ones were already burned into her mind; so why did those tales have to be continuously retold?

Sarain closed her eyes and thought; she would have to remember the happy memories on her own. She struggled to think of the curves of his face, and the way it looked when he smiled at her; what it felt like to be near him, and the way her heart raced when he would enter the room. She never felt more alive than when she was burning with that childhood crush.

Orran...

Chapter 5

Sarain held her sword up to block his blade; Orran was teaching her how to sword fight. She was barely thirteen, but her grandfather was expecting her to master the technique of sword fighting soon, a feat that sixteen year old Orran had already done. Orran swung his blade at Sarain and she successfully blocked him again. It seemed as though she was doing well, but she knew that he was taking it easy on her, he always did. She ran at him and swung her sword towards Orran who quickly dodged the strike. It was like he didn't even have to try.

Sarain stopped and lowered her blade. Orran noted her lack of effort and asked, "Why are you stopping?"

"What's the point? You're not giving it your all. How am I going to get any better if you don't challenge me?" Sarain stated to him.

"You're not ready for that yet," he simply replied.

"How can you be sure if you don't let me try?" she questioned.

"You could get hurt," he answered.

"You wouldn't hurt me," she responded, looking him in the eyes.

Orran gazed at her for a moment, and then finally said, "Alright."

Sarain raised her sword once again, and Orran did not waste a second, he charged her immediately, moving faster than she had expected. She dove out of the way, throwing her sword aside. Then she swiftly rolled to the blade and picked it up, jumping to her feet. Orran was charging again and in the middle of a swing with his sword. Sarain hoisted her blade up into the air and it clanged hard against Orran's steel. The sword shook in her hands as Orran forced his weight down on the blade. She gripped on the hilt tighter, trying to keep from having her sword forced out of her hands. Her fingers ached and her hands were turning red under the pressure, but she held on. And as if realizing that she wasn't going to let up, Orran quickly changed his tactic and spun around Sarain. He grabbed her by the waist, catching her off guard, and making her drop her sword.

Orran leaned down to Sarain's ear, his arms still wrapped around her, and whispered, "If I had been a real enemy and swung at you; you would be dead."

Sarain turned around to face Orran, she gazed up at him, and said, "Then I'm lucky that you're not an enemy."

Orran stared down at her with his hazel eyes. Sarain took a deep breath and suddenly started to feel like this wasn't about training anymore. She looked up at him nervously, she had been close to Orran before while sparring, but this was different. Her heart was beating rapidly, she had always liked him, but she thought that he had only ever seen her as a kid that followed him around. Now standing there in his arms, Sarain was beginning to believe that maybe Orran was seeing her differently.

He leaned down towards her and she started to stretch up, all the while looking at his lips, but they both stopped and pulled away when a voice called out "Sarain" from nearby. It was her grandfather, looking for her for more training.

Sarain glanced over at Orran, but he avoided her gaze, and was looking embarrassed. Her grandfather was now approaching, unaware of what he had just broken up. He stopped in front of Orran and instructed him to take care of some of the clan's chores, and Orran began to leave. Sarain watched him walk away, and hoped that he would look back at her one last time, but he didn't.

Sarain looked up at Delmar and waited for her own instructions, all the while feeling angry at him having sent Orran away. He was always ordering Orran around, given he was the chief, but it was like he was always going harder on him. But Orran never complained he just did as he was told. He would never do anything to disrespect the chief.

Sarain spent the day studying the hunter's handbook and trying to make sense of the water damaged pages, but it wasn't going well. The ink had bled so much so that it was almost gone, and the water had made the indentations from writing on the pages nearly nonexistent. Finally she gave up and put the book down, and instead dressed for tonight's hunt. She would have to hunt alone since Eddie was scheduled to work a late shift. She was both glad and disappointed to be hunting alone; she found herself able to move more freely without Eddie to look out for, but she was also growing accustomed to having him around.

She covered her skin in black, and was soon out the door. The sky was already dark for awhile by the time Sarain left her home, but she wasn't worried. She no longer feared being tracked back, since many demons in town already knew of her, and some even knew of her residence. And most of them knew well enough to leave her alone, and those that didn't were usually the weaker kind that wouldn't pose much of a threat anyway. No demon could get inside with the barriers, and none were bold enough to try to burn her place down. Sarain had become something of a legend there amongst the demon kind that served as a warning for them to not step out of line, or to at least stay hidden.

She hadn't really come across any strong demons in awhile, just a steady wave of amateurs; nothing like her days against Sephor. The demons at the X were the closest thing to a threat, but her partnership with them helped her keep a close watchful eye over them.

Sarain did wonder about the couple who killed James' kids, this Cyrus and Desmina. It was a bold move that they should have known would get back to her, if they were from around there, but she had never heard of them till then, and nothing had popped up since. James had also not turned up yet, but Sarain wasn't surprised, she figured he would want to get lost after losing his children.

Sarain walked the shadowy streets, they were mostly empty except for the occasional car or couple who thought a late night stroll might be romantic. Sarain thought how much of a mood killer it would be for one of these couples to get attacked by a demon while on their walk, well maybe it wasn't a mood killer for her and Eddie, but it definitely would be to someone without experience in fighting them. Though it also occurred to Sarain that that was why she was out hunting, to stop these creatures and protect these innocent people, so that they could hopefully lead the normal life that Sarain could not.

The air was quiet, and cooler than it had been in a while. Sarain still hadn't come across any creatures yet, and this was beginning to become a habit. Lately she had noticed that the number of violent demons was dwindling. While The X's vil sang business was still okay, the full blooded demons seemed to be disappearing, and the vil sangs weren't a problem. Sarain had been considering that perhaps it was time she moved on from this city, and it was a notion that she hadn't brought up with Eddie. In fact, he was the real reason she had stayed there so long, whether she was ready to admit it to herself or not. Sarain wasn't sure what she should do, she didn't like letting her personal feelings factor into her work, but that didn't stop it from happening.

Sarain's focus was taken as soon as she heard a rustle come from the bushes a few yards ahead of her. Though it was shadowy, her eyes made out a dark figure inside the already dark shrubbery. It stood there watching and waiting and Sarain wondered if the thing truly thought that she couldn't see it. She didn't feel like waiting for it to make the first move, so she started towards it while beginning to unsheathe her blade. Red eyes suddenly flashed from inside the bushes, and the creature came rushing out, realizing that it had been spotted and now coming out full force. The demon was a different breed than Sarain was used to seeing; it had slick black fur instead of scales, but the rest of its structure was the same. Fur or scales made no difference to her, except she liked the idea that her blade would easily slice through fur much more quickly than a hard hide.

Sarain swung at the beast, but it dodged her attack; it was quicker than she anticipated, the fur probably made it lighter than the demons she usually fought. This wasn't a problem, she was holding back anyway. The creature hissed at her, and it reminded her of a cat. It leapt at her, but Sarain moved more swiftly and swung at the beast again. The creature broke in two, its hind legs dropped instantly, while its torso continued to fly forward until it finally landed a couple of yards away. It was dead before its body hit the ground. The whole thing felt kind of anti-climactic to Sarain; she had expected a better fight out of it. She was surprised that she was able to slice it in half with one swing; she had underestimated her own strength.

Sarain walked over to the torso and bent down to give it a closer look. The creature's face still had the expression of a growl on it; its blood stained teeth were exposed and glistened with saliva. It almost looked like an animal close to a dog, rather than a demon, but it had the same broad brow line, the same clawed three fingered hands, and its ears were pointed and molded closely to its head, all of which were common demon traits. Sarain found it interesting to see a different kind of demon. They were like animals, and came in breeds. Even the vil sangs could be different, some looking demonic, some human. Whatever the face may be, it was the blood that drove the creature, causing it to wreak havoc.

Sarain stood back up, but then something out the corner of her eye caught her attention, a shadow moved behind her. She quickly spun around, but the grassy field behind her was empty. Trees lightly swayed in the gentle breeze, perhaps one of them had been playing with her vision. Her eyes still searched the area, scanning for anything out of place, but there was nothing.

Sarain turned back around, glanced down quickly at the remains again, and then headed off to continue her walk. She placed her blade back in its sheath at her side, and strolled down the street, peacefully walking. Hunting and killing demons were a routine for Sarain, and it was one that barely broke her concentration now. Eddie often made jokes that she could probably kill demons in her sleep, but really, the idea wasn't too farfetched.

Sarain worked her way deeper into the city. She started down the narrow alleyways and headed towards the city's slums, prime hunting grounds. But pickings were still slim; the demons didn't appear to want to play tonight.

Sarain trekked for hours, but all she found were a few everyday lowlifes; not the monsters she was looking for. The end of the night was growing near, and dawn was approaching. She began to make her way back home, she started by cutting through a small alley behind a bar; not the best place for a pretty lady. The alley was cluttered with trash: paper, bottles, and boxes. Debris was piled up high. Sarain started down the alley. Her footsteps thumped loudly on the concrete, her steps normally didn't make a sound. As her first step sounded down the alley, the noise of her movement caused a pile of trash to suddenly shift. Sarain hesitated; perhaps it was an animal or maybe a human, with it being so close to dawn the demons should have already gone into hiding. Still, Sarain proceeded with caution.

She took another loud step, even with trying to walk softly, though this time the trash didn't move. Sarain knew what she had seen, there was definitely something hiding within the pile of trash. She began to draw out her machete, but was hesitating to use it in case the creature turned out to be a harmless animal or a drunken human.

She slowly approached the pile of debris, and at first thought to stab it with her blade, but refrained from doing so. Instead, she kicked at the trash, and her foot hit something solid within it. Sarain kicked it again after the first time resulted in no reaction; this time she kicked with much more force which resulted with a groaning sound coming from inside the pile of trash.

The debris shifted once again, and Sarain readied her blade. The object was big, and undoubtedly not an animal, its size and reaction gave it away. It had to be a person.

"Get out of there, you drunk. This is no place to sleep it off," Sarain shouted towards the pile. She grabbed at a large flattened box that she thought may have been covering the person's head. She pulled the debris away and revealed a grimy drunken man who was still clinging to a glass bottle wrapped in a brown paper bag. The man's hair looked clumped and matted, it was brown but she could tell it had once been sandy blond and was now covered in filth. She knew this only because she recognized the man, but he had changed a lot in the days it had been since she had last seen him. The light that had been in his eyes was gone, along with any hope of happiness.

Sarain looked down at him with sympathy, and said, "James... You shouldn't be here."

Chapter 6

"James, what are you doing?" Sarain asked with concern.

He looked up at her with his green eyes glazed over and replied, "Not feeling so much."

"If you stay out here any longer you won't be feeling anything anymore," Sarain made comment to the imminent sunrise.

"Does it even really matter? It'd be just one less vil sang for you to kill, right?" James stated sourly.

Sarain sighed as she bent down and said to him, "I have no reason to kill you, besides, we still need to find your children's killers. Do you really wish for them to go un-avenged?"

"I can't stop them, and it wouldn't bring my kids back," he muttered.

"So you're giving up?" Sarain asked with a crude tone of voice. She let a moment go by for him to respond, but he didn't, instead he avoided her gaze, and began to raise his bottle to his lips. Before James could get a drink, Sarain snatched the bottle out of his hands. He reached for the bottle and Sarain threw it to the ground with force causing it to shatter to pieces and its potent liquid spraying over the concrete.

"Stop being so damned weak!" she shouted at him.

"I don't want to!" he yelled back.

Sarain looked up at the sky, and then turned back to James and said, "It's almost dawn, you have to get inside!" But James made no effort to move; finally an infuriated Sarain grabbed him by the arm and yanked him up.

James howled in pain and cried out, "My arm!" But Sarain didn't let go, she continued to pull him down the alley, looking around for a quick place to hide him. She wasn't in the business of stashing vil sangs, and didn't have a place in mind. Her home was too far away, and the barrier within its frame would keep him out anyway.

They shuffled out the alley, but a shadow from behind her, still in the alley, caught Sarain's attention. She looked over, but saw nothing. She couldn't waste any more time, she had to assume it was nothing, and leave the thought behind.

Sarain dragged a helpless James, who was both too tired and too drunk to resist her. They were still in the slummy part of the city when the sun began coming up. James began to scream and Sarain quickly kicked in the boarded up door of an abandoned building and threw him inside. James landed hard against the ground; he cried out and grabbed at his arm. Sarain ignored his cries and looked around; the building was dark and boarded up enough so that sunlight shouldn't get in.

Finally she knelt down and glanced over the arm James was complaining over. It hung limply to his side, and Sarain realized that she had dislocated it. She placed her hand on the back of his shoulder and told him, "This is going to hurt." Before James had time to react to her statement, Sarain immediately snapped his shoulder back in place, and he hollered in agony.

"Sorry about that," Sarain said with little sympathy in her voice, and then she added, "You're going to have to stay here for the day."

"So that's your great plan, abuse an already beaten man, and then strand him helplessly alone knowing he longs to die?" James stated half amused.

Sarain stepped aside and spoke bluntly, "If you really want to die then by all means, step outside." James stared up at her, blankly, for a moment, and then Sarain continued to say, "Really it shouldn't take very long for you to catch fire, and I would imagine a few seconds of pure agony should be worth an eternity of nothingness afterward."

"You don't believe in heaven?" he asked her.

"I don't believe in it for demons. Besides, a perfect world of happiness just sounds like wishful thinking," she blurted out; Sarain wasn't an optimist.

A sad expression began to form on James' face, and Sarain commented, "Did I spoil your hopes for a happy ending?" She wasn't meaning to be crude, but everything she was saying kept coming out that way.

But then surprising James answered, "No, or at least not the way you think. I understand thinking that there would be no heaven for a vil sang like me, but for you to think there would be no heaven for someone like yourself, doing God's work and all. Well that is what I find sad."

"I don't do God's work, I only do my own. Why should I do anything for someone who has done nothing for me? When I kill demons, that's because I'm the one who wants them dead," she explained with intensity in her voice.

"But God gave you life," James pressed on.

"No, my mother gave me life. And that life isn't one that should be praised, or one that someone should feel grateful for. Even you having had a true life with a family, no matter how poorly it has turned, is still one that is better than my own. You sulk because you lost your children, but you should be grateful for ever even having them," Sarain scolded him, her voice beginning to shake with emotion.

James got quiet, and suddenly felt as though a nerve had been hit, he could tell Sarain was being affected by more than what was going on with himself, and he wasn't prepared to dive into the issues she had buried down. Instead he simply answered, "You're right."

They were both silent for a while until Sarain finally spoke by saying, "Now if you're feeling calmer, I have to go get some sleep. Can I leave you here alone?"

"I'll be fine," he replied, gazing up at her, thinking of how quickly she was able to both fly off the handle and then suddenly seem compassionate.

"Good. I'll come back at dusk to check on you," she said.

"I'll be here," James remarked while watching as Sarain started to leave. He wasn't quite sure if he meant what he said, but looking at Sarain, he did know that he wanted to see her again.

Sarain stepped out into the sun, it was a bright and beautiful morning, but Sarain just felt tired and wanted sleep. She thought of Eddie, wondering how his night had been, and then began to wonder if James was really planning on staying put. It would be his decision; she wasn't going to babysit him. She wasn't really sure why she had even made as much effort as she had to help him, he was still a vil sang. Perhaps she just felt sorry for him. Either way, she honestly planned to go back to check on him after having had some rest.

Sarain made her long walk home, and was happy when she finally arrived. She went straight to her bedroom, only stopping briefly to glance at the mirror on the wall, making sure it reflected nothing out of the norm. Just she shown back, an amazement itself for her. She liked a mirror that made her feel normal, and was beginning to see why people liked them so much, given her reasons were much different from theirs.

Sarain then went to her bed and collapsed immediately on it. She was tired from her long night, which had been more of a glorified hike than a hunt. Her eyes gazed over at the mirror one last time before drifting off to sleep. She thought of her grandfather, and how she thought she had seen him in the mirror. Delmar had always watched over her, but his watchful eye very rarely felt like one of a caring guardian, but more of someone waiting for Sarain to make a mistake, and his discipline was harsh.

Delmar could be a tyrant, but he had been the only family Sarain had to learn from. She was curious as to how much of her personality came from him. She had once been a joyful spirited child; she wondered when exactly it was that Delmar broke her.

Sarain continued to watch as Orran walked away, before Delmar finally cleared his throat and said, "I think it best you don't let yourself get distracted from your studies; you will practice only with me from now on."

Sarain looked up at her grandfather in shock and pleaded, "That's not fair! Orran is a great trainer."

"Maybe, but I don't want him teaching you anything more than the art of combat," Delmar stated with a firm tone of voice.

"What's that supposed to mean?" Sarain got defensive.

"You know what I mean; I'm not blind. If he was teaching as well as he should, you two wouldn't be as chummy as the two of you act. Real training brings out fury, and that kind of fury doesn't easily go away after a spar," he explained to her.

"That's ridiculous, I'm perfectly able to separate practice from my everyday life. I don't need to hate Orran to be a good fighter," she defended.

Delmar glared down at her, and then gave her a smug smirk, and said, "Fine, you want to continue training with Orran then you'll have to prove that he has been training you well. If you can hold your own in a short, let's say, two minute match with me, then I will let you continue studying under Orran. And if not, then you will no longer train with anyone other than me."

Sarain glared back at her grandfather, and simply nodded her head in agreement feeling that if she spoke than she wouldn't be able to keep herself from expressing what she really thought about him. She was tired of Delmar constantly pushing her to work harder; over and over again he would press her to her limits, never letting her rest. For just one moment Sarain wanted to live the life of a child, and get to do the things that normal teenagers got to do. And she was always wondering how things would have been different if her mother had lived. But her mother wasn't there; Sarain had only herself to rely on, and the only way her grandfather would take her seriously, is if she bested him in a fight. She only had to remain standing for her to win their bet, but she wanted more. She wanted to take him down.

Sarain picked up her sword and readied her stance as Delmar prepared himself. She held her blade up almost as if she were going to rest it on her shoulder. Delmar observed her position then shook his head, but said nothing. Instead, he stood with his sword pointed outward. Finally he looked to her and nodded his head.

Sarain hesitated for a second, unsure if her grandfather had given her the go ahead to fight or was telling her to change her position. His eyes glared over at her, and he finally shouted, "Go!" Sarain's question was answered.

She rushed Delmar quickly, but he just as quick moved out of her path, dodging the attack. Sarain spun around, and swung at her grandfather, but her blade's stride was nowhere close to hitting him. She didn't want to actually hit him, since this was only a practice, but she had hoped to scare him or even impress him so that she could win the fight. Sarain ran at him once more and again at the last possible moment, Delmar moved out of the way. The fact that he was avoiding her without any real effort and that he hadn't even attempted to charge her was only making Sarain angrier. It was like he was letting her win, but the fact that he was the one making it happen made it feel more like a loss to Sarain. She wondered if he was just toying with her; waiting for her to let her guard down before he would attack.

Time was running out, and while Sarain still stood, by Delmar's terms, in her own eyes she had done nothing worthy enough to win the fight. She felt herself growing frustrated and glared back at her grandfather. She matched the look that was in his eyes, she knew her grandfather took himself very seriously, but the way he looked at her seemed more like an expression of hate than one of discipline. He was always staring at her with that glint in his eyes; a glint of disapproval, and maybe even a glint of disgust; as if she could never be the warrior he wanted her to be, and it was as though he had already given up on her before trying.

Sarain began to feel sad, and then her anger turned to sorrow. She would always be a disappointment to him; she was not the best student of the clan, and she could never replace her mother, his real daughter. She was just a second rate substitute, that was what the look in his eyes told her.

Sarain stopped and lowered her sword. Delmar stared at her, puzzled, and shouted, "What are you doing? Time isn't up!"

"It doesn't matter, you win," Sarain stated, she knew there was nothing she could do to change his mind, nothing to impress him, nothing to get his approval. Why try? She thought to herself.

To Sarain's surprise, she looked up to see Delmar charging at her. She had assumed that he had put down his sword, but instead he was coming at her full force, and he was furious. Sarain quickly raised her sword to block his attack, their blades clanged together loudly, and Delmar immediately swung again. Sarain barely jumped out of its path, but his blade had come close to hitting her, too close. She was beginning to think that Delmar was no longer practicing with her, but actually trying to hurt her. Did he really hate her that much?

Sarain blocked another one of his attacks with her sword, but this time instead of swinging again, her grandfather began to force his weight down on to his sword. It was the same tactic Orran had used on her earlier during their training session, but Delmar was a bigger man, and the weight of his sword was more than Sarain could stand. Her sword was forced out of her hands, and fell with a heavy thud to the ground. It was obvious that she had lost, but Delmar didn't stop there. Sarain was still standing, and in attempt to degrade her, he kicked her in the stomach, causing her to collapse to the ground. He wanted her down, by his terms.

Sarain gasped for air while on the ground, having had the breath knocked out of her. Delmar lowered his sword as he stood beside her, staring down at her, and then he stated, "The fight is not over when you say it's over. It's over when you're the last one standing."

He left her there on the dirt, still gasping, and it was a while before Sarain managed to help herself up. She picked up her sword to put it away, but the act of bending to reach for it sent shockwaves of pain throughout her body. Her stomach felt badly bruised, and she soon realized that she could barely even walk.

She understood that her grandfather was trying to make her a stronger fighter, but she hated him for it. And she was truly beginning to feel that he hated her as well.

Chapter 7

Sarain opened her eyes, and groggily blinked them, trying to shake out the darkness. After a moment, she realized that it wasn't her, but that it was in fact the room that was dark. She looked at the clock by her bedside. It was after seven, she had slept past dusk, and for more than twelve hours. She had never done that before.

Sarain sat up and still felt tired. The room had a haze about it, and it took her a minute to realize why. Then Sarain noticed that the mirror was glowing, its normally black glass now looked like an illuminated silver. Only the reflective glass glowed, its frame remained the same, but even the glass alone was enough to worry Sarain. She was regretting having brought it in her home, and was beginning to see why it had been so different from other mirrors. While it worked for her like ordinary mirrors worked for regular people, it was still a very abnormal object. And after another moment of staring in awe, Sarain learned what else made the mirror so special. She hadn't dreamt the first incident unless she was dreaming at that very moment, because she saw her grandfather once more, watching out from within the mirror. His dark eyes stared back, and the same stern expression was upon his face that she remembered always being there.

Sarain slowly stood up and walked closer to the mirror, but she remained with a bit of distance from it, worried that perhaps something might jump out at her from it. Delmar's eyes followed her movements silently, but he seemed fully aware of her presence. She stared at his image, almost frightened by it; not sure if she was glad to see her grandfather, or scared by the thought that something else could be masquerading as him.

Finally she inched herself closer, and then a look of realization came over Delmar's face. "Sarain?" his voice echoed out of the mirror. The voice sounded familiar, but at the same time it didn't sound normal. It sounded static-y and as though the voice was made up of vibrations. Sarain was hesitant to get closer or even to answer. When she neared enough for her eyes to catch the light coming off of the mirror, Delmar seemed to gasp.

"Sarain, it is you," he spoke out, almost sounding happy. It was a tone she couldn't remember hearing him use. She continued to keep her distance. She wasn't sure if this entity was truly her grandfather; this mirror had after all been in the possession of two demonic vil sangs, it may be an object of evil trying to trick her into letting it out.

She remained quiet and moved no further. Delmar took notice and then asked, "Do you not recognize me?"

Sarain decided to answer by saying, "I see my grandfather's image, but I don't know for sure who I am looking at."

"I am the same man you once knew, not a shape-shifting phantom," he stated, but that wasn't enough for Sarain. She questioned him, distrusting the image, by saying, "My real grandfather wouldn't have me be so trusting, and he'd want me to make him prove himself."

"Yes, that's right, that's what I would have you do," Delmar acknowledged, almost seeming glad this time, "Ask me then something only I should know."

Sarain scanned her brain both thinking of what to ask and what some dark entity might say to try to trick her. Then a memory popped into her head, and she glared back at her grandfather's image and asked, "What did you do when my mother died?"

A solemn expression came over his face, and it was obvious that it wasn't a question he wanted to hear. The room stood silent, and Sarain waited rather impatiently for him to answer. "Answer the question," she pressed him, raising her voice to the man she once feared.

His eyes looked tearful, as if he were experiencing the pain he had caused her. He finally replied by saying, "I left you alone."

"No, before that," she said with a menacing tone.

"I told you to stop crying," Delmar weakly choked out.

"No, you yelled at me to stop crying, and said that my weakness made you sick," Sarain declared back, a tear escaping her eye, she afterward hushing-ly added, "Then you left me alone."

A tear escaped Delmar's eye as well and he told her, "I'm so sorry for that... I'm sorry for a lot of things... I'm not that same man anymore, but I am your grandfather."

"You may be my grandfather, but you died a long time ago, and I don't need you now," she stated. Sarain then turned and walked out of the room. She had thought many times over what she might do or say if she could ever see her grandfather again, in her mind he was always glad to see her, that he would tell her how proud of her he was, and then they would embrace. But somewhere along the line that dream died, and only the bitter memories were left. Sarain had just turned her back on the man who raised her, and perhaps the only chance to make a connection to the spirit world. So many questions she had, and so many possible answers he could give her, but none of them seemed so important that she would ask them from that man.

Why couldn't God send her someone else?

Sarain sat in her bathroom for fifteen minutes, thinking of the past, and of other things she could have said, before finally coming out and going back to her bedroom where the mirror hung. The mirror no longer glowed nor reflected her grandfather. The room was dark, and the mirror was black again and had returned to reflecting her own image. She had wondered why the mirror didn't reflect her memories the way others did; now she realized it was because it would reflect them in a different way, by capturing those who only lived in her memories, and allowing her to speak with them again.

Sarain stared at the mirror, doubting her sanity, and still questioning if she had just imagined the whole thing. Why did it have to be her grandfather? He wasn't the man she longed to speak to.

Suddenly something came to her, a memory of a different kind. James. She had forgotten to meet him. She had left him alone in that abandoned building promising to return, and here it was hours past dusk and she had failed to keep her word. She looked at the clock and thought, perhaps he was still waiting, but she would have to hurry.

Sarain quickly dressed and rushed out the door. She didn't own a car and went everywhere on foot, except for the occasional bus ride, which was more for when she wasn't "working". She hurried tonight, but waiting for a bus would take more time, and Sarain on foot was quicker than that. She didn't bother hunting for demons, or really even keeping out a watchful eye; all these took time that she couldn't afford to lose.

Sarain wasn't sure why she cared enough to hurry. Yes, she was one to keep her word, that was important to her, but she wasn't someone to make such promises to vil sangs. Still, she felt sorry for James, he had lost his children, and though it wasn't her fault, she still held herself accountable for not keeping a better watch of the city. She was the one to let two violent demonic vil sangs slip by, and allowing them to take his children. She had discussed this with Eddie before; actually, it was more Eddie talking, and reassuring that she couldn't possibly know everything that was happening in the city; all of its problems couldn't be dealt with by one person. And he was right, but then he was always saying things to try and comfort her.

The familiar alley behind the bar came into view; it was where Sarain had found James the previous night, the abandoned building she left him in wasn't far from there. Her quick footsteps pounded loudly on the concrete as she rushed down the alley. The building was just ahead, Sarain could see its boarded door that she had kicked in still laying on the ground. She ran to it, and caught herself as she reached the doorway. Her long hair swished behind her, and she realized she had forgotten to tie it back. She peered in only to see darkness, yet wondered if James could still be inside. She stepped in, and suddenly realized that she was unarmed, she had forgotten to bring a weapon in her hurry. It was a mistake she had never made before. Sarain tried not to be angry with herself; telling herself that it was only James, she didn't need a weapon, though it being night, and this being an abandoned property, anything could be there by now.

The open room was both dark and quiet. Old junk that had been left behind from its previous days of use now cluttered the room. Sarain searched the place both on foot and with her eyes, scanning the room for movement and any signs of James' presence. The building was empty, except for a few rodents, which wouldn't help her find James. Sarain didn't know where else to look, James had always come to her, and she didn't know where he resided. She didn't feel right about leaving such a desperate and hopeless man alone. James could be anywhere, and could have done anything. Either way, he wasn't there, and Sarain needed to either get inside or find a weapon; she was a strong warrior, but given the right demon at the wrong time, she may find herself out matched.

Sarain headed for the door, and upon exiting, a shadow further down the alley caught her attention. It loomed long and still, but the source of the shadow could not be seen. Sarain was sure that such a shadow had not been there earlier when she passed through that section of the alley, and being unarmed, she wasn't prepared to take that way back. She would have to continue down the alleyway in the direction she had been going, and take a longer detoured route back home. She took long steady strides, but didn't move too quickly. She wanted to keep her own steps quiet so that she could hear if anyone else's would follow hers.

The air echoed only her own steps, and she began to feel at ease. A cool breeze blew through, blowing back her dark hair, and as Sarain made her way down the alley, the sound of a faint thud brought a chill to her spine. The thud was then followed by another and another. Sarain didn't need to turn around to know that the footsteps were coming from the alleyway behind her; whatever had made the looming shadow was now on the move and following her.

She hurried her steps, and the follower soon matched her pace. It sounded as though the stalker was trying to match their steps with the echo of hers so as to not be heard by her, but Sarain could tell that the steps did not hold the same sound. Not only were the steps slightly off, but the shift sound in weight was also wrong, the second steps sounded heavier than her own, and definitely much too heavy to be the sounds of an echo.

This wasn't a game that Sarain wanted to play, and she wasn't about to let this thing get the upper hand. If it wanted to capture her then it would have to be quick enough to catch her. Sarain took off in a full pace run, her feet pounding against the ground loudly, and was followed by the sound of another pair scampering after her. As she ran she caught sight of a garbage can ahead of her, and when she reached it, she grabbed a hold of the metal barrel and threw it to the ground causing it to noisily clang against the concrete and clutter the alleyway behind her. She heard the footsteps stop once they reached the trashcan, and then she heard nothing after that.

It couldn't be that easy, she thought to herself, but Sarain continued to race forward, until she saw the end of the alley come into sight, and a wide open street that it exited to that would give her a very public view. A demon wouldn't dare chase her out into such an open area where it could become exposed. It was just a few feet ahead, yet each step felt excruciatingly long.

With a gasp, Sarain ran right out into the street, barely being missed by a speeding car, whose driver immediately slammed down on their horn, which was then followed by the driver shouting obscenities out of their window at her. The car didn't stop; the driver didn't seem to care why Sarain would be so desperate to run out into the road, only that they had been inconvenienced by her.

Sarain stopped, still in the road, but with no other cars coming. Across the street from her was a coffee shop with large glass windows; lights and people could be seen inside, a few of the patrons stared out at her to see what the commotion was. Sarain felt safe that the area was public enough; the creature shouldn't follow her out of the alley. But as she turned around to look back towards the alley, her eyes grew wide and her mouth gaped open as she was shocked to see a man lunging out at her from the alleyway with a large knife in hand. He knocked her to the ground, where she fell down onto her back.

Sarain gasped for air, as she struggled to get a hold of the man while he raised his blade in the air, preparing to slash her. One of her hands grabbed at the man's throat before she realized that he had stopped his own hand. And it took her a moment to notice what the man had already seen; staring back at her, in the eyes of the stranger, was the same rich shade of violet that was in her own.

Chapter 8

The man stared down at Sarain, still pinning her down, but with confusion in his face. He continued to hold his blade, but made no attempt to use it. The stranger simply stared down at Sarain studying her face and focusing on her eyes.

Sarain too was surprised, but her instinct for survival was still intact, and the second she realized that the man's guard was down, she quickly shoved him off her and sprung up to her feet.

The stranger flew back and landed hard on the ground before Sarain realized how hard she had thrown him. He groaned as he slowly got up, the knife was missing from his grasp, and Sarain quickly started scanning the street with her eyes for it. It must have been thrown when she shoved the man, and as she searched for it the thought came to her mind, "Why would a vil sang need a knife?" His slowness getting up was also pointing to the likeliness that he wasn't a demon, but his eyes, they were only normal for her...unless.

The man began to approach Sarain, regardless of the fact that she had just injured him, and still looking just as baffled as before. His mouth began to open, and the first thought that popped into Sarain's mind was, was he going to have fangs? But instead, it was a normal set of teeth and the words, "What is this?" that echoed out.

Sarain didn't know how to answer, mostly because she didn't know what he was asking. But then the stranger made himself very clear when he simply said one word, "Ariana?"

Sarain's heart felt like it had stopped beating when she heard him say that name, and then she understood why the man had froze from the mere sight of her. It was so obvious that she was surprised she didn't see it sooner. This man wasn't a vil sang or a crazed stalker, he was her father.

Sarain stared blankly at the man, and replied, "She was my mother." The man's expression went vacant, and Sarain gave him a minute to take in what he had just heard. The man stood there looking lost in thought, and only breaking his focus to take in glances of Sarain, as though looking for the resemblance.

After a while he finally broke the silence by saying, "And to think, I thought you were a vil sang."

"Why would you think that?" Sarain asked curiously, almost insulted that someone could make the mistake of labeling her a demon.

"I got a tip that someone had seen a vil sang holding up in one of the abandoned buildings in the area. So when I saw a pale young woman coming out of one of the buildings, unarmed none the less, I figured there was no other logical reason you'd be there, unless you were a vil sang. Pretty girls don't usually wander in dangerous areas unless they are dangerous themselves," he answered.

Sarain thought of James, and the fact that someone must have seen him if word got back to this man, her father. Perhaps that's why he didn't stay put to wait for her. Sarain pondered over what the man had told her, and then another question came to mind, "So you're a demon hunter? My mother never told me that."

"Well, I'm not surprised that you wouldn't know much about me, since I didn't know about you, but yes, I do hunt, which I assume you do as well, given your family's background," he replied, his voice steady and strong.

"It's what I was taught to do when they were around, which is more than I can say for you," she stated with a bit of anger in her tone.

"The clan your family was a part of wasn't big on keeping company with rogue hunters; we were only kept around as long as we were useful and when our skills or knowledge was no longer needed, we were cut loose. They didn't give any other option to it, but I guess that is no excuse for letting them separate me from your mother," he reminisced.

Sarain stared at him, unsure of how genuine he was, or if he was merely trying to save face with her. She had many questions to ask him, but couldn't once they were interrupted by the loud sounds of sirens approaching. They both turned and looked towards the noise to see lights flashing.

"Someone must have called the cops when they saw us fighting," her father commented, and before Sarain could react, he moved forward and grabbed her by the arm. He tugged on her arm, and quickly said, "Come with me, we need to get out of here."

They dashed into the alley and raced back down into it. Sarain doubted that the cops would follow; especially when they would learn that no one was hurt, but she did wonder if Eddie was one of the cops to respond to the call.

Sarain followed her father through the alley, past the abandoned building she had hidden James in, and into the bar she had found him behind. Sarain had a feeling that her father's tip had come from someone inside there.

They sat down in a small booth towards the back of the bar, away from the other customers. The place was dimly lit and hardly occupied. It wasn't the kind of bar a person would go to for a good time, it was more a place to get lost at. Sarain noticed that she was the only woman inside, and also the youngest one there. Others noticed as well since Sarain was catching a number of stares from the older men. She ignored it and focused her attention on her father, and a conversation she had only ever dreamed of having.

She looked him in his eyes, still amazed that they were also violet, and asked him a question she had always wondered, "Why are our eyes purple?"

Her father smiled at her, as though not surprised that she would ask, and he answered, "It's actually a rare family genetic mutation, but it dominates in our blood.

Something is wrong with one of our chromosomes that effects our pigmentation, but for some reason it's only visible in our eyes. I don't know the full science behind it, but it's been around for generations."

"Why are you here in town?" Sarain wondered, a little suspicious of the coincidence of running into her father.

"Same reason as you, I imagine, I'm here to hunt," he simply replied, and then he added after a silent moment went by, "Was there anything else you wanted to ask?"

Another revelation suddenly came to Sarain, another that should have been more obvious if she hadn't been over thinking so hard, and she asked, "What is your name?"

He looked shocked by her question, then a sad look came over his face, and he said, "She really didn't tell you anything about me, did she... My name is Aion... I guess I should ask you yours."

"It's Sarain," she answered, thinking of how this wasn't the normal kind of conversation one would have with a parent or a total stranger. He was her father, the same blood flowed through their veins, and still he was a stranger, and being so made her unable to shake off the urge to keep her guard up around him. As she sat there Sarain neither felt a bond nor a real connection with Aion more than their odd eye color. She knew that a bond would come in time, but she had always imagined feeling some kind of relief if she had ever met her father, like a kind of safety, but with Aion, she felt nothing.

He glanced at her strangely, as if reading her thoughts and knowing her troubles, and he stated, "This is just as strange for me. I went from being alone to having a daughter all in one day."

Sarain tried to give Aion a smile, but it came out as a weak awkward smirk; there was still more bothering her. One thing she had to know and found herself saying aloud was, "Did you love my mother?"

"More than anything," Aion replied with sadness in his tone, "I never wanted to let her go, but when I went to get her to take her with me, I found that the clan had moved. I'm sure it was her father's doing, the man had never approved of me, but the fact that she had went with him without so much as a word, told me that my feelings weren't as returned as I had believed."

"And you didn't try to find her?" Sarain asked, still not quite satisfied with his response.

"Her clan could get lost if they truly wanted to, and I had figured she didn't want to be found by me. Maybe it was wrong of me to think so, but I was also a wounded man back then," Aion answered with a sound of regret.

Memories began to flood back to Sarain, and she debated whether or not to tell them to her father. Looking at the man sitting across from her, his solemn disposition and the feeling of emptiness coming off him, led Sarain to believe that her thoughts could only help him find some kind of inner peace. So she spoke of what she recalled, "I remember, anytime I would ever ask about you, my mother would get sad, like she regretted something. And though she would never speak of you, she did once say that I was conceived in love."

Aion smiled, and then looked away from her. Sarain believed she given him a happy moment, but the aura he put off was still a sad one. His expression then turned serious once more and he turned back and asked her, "And what did your grandfather say of me?"

"He didn't, he forbid me to talk of you," Sarain spoke in a tense tone.

"And your mother allowed him to do this?" he asked with astonishment.

"No, this was after she died," she explained, confused by his confusion.

"He raised you?" Aion spoke even more astounded.

"Yes, until the attack," Sarain slowly said while reading Aion's expression, and with her observation of him she deduced, "You really did lose track of the clan, didn't you. You know nothing of their destruction?"

He closed his eyes, an appearance of failure came over his face, and then he simply asked, "When?"

"Ten years ago," Sarain told him, he let out a short and hushed gasp, making her also think to say, "My mother died eight years earlier."

Aion opened eyes and stared at Sarain and immediately asked her, "Who raised you after that?"

"…No one, it was just me," she said, emotionless. Aion looked as though he was going to tear up, but Sarain felt no emotion by it, she was only speaking of things that had already passed, and it was a fact she had since learned to live with.

Aion reached out for Sarain's hand, but she quickly moved it away; not out of hate, but out of the inexperience to an emotional situation. She didn't understand that Aion was seeking both comfort and to comfort her. He didn't react to her lack of wanting to be touched, but he did continue to grieve by telling her, "I'm so sorry, you don't know what I would have done to be there."

"It doesn't matter now, the past can't be changed, and you couldn't help not knowing of me," Sarain said trying to be kind.

Aion nodded in agreement, and then a look of realization came over his face and he looked at her and asked, "How did you survive?"

"I hid," Sarain answered quickly; it was partly true, but she didn't know how to explain how she had managed to kill one demon with her bare hands and was then left to live by the rest. It was something that she herself could never understand, and no one else would believe.

"Last call, time to close out tabs!" the bartender called out, it broke them both away from their conversation. Sarain quickly looked at a clock hanging on the wall to see that it was nearly two a.m. Aion turned and gazed at his daughter, and asked, "Should we go someplace else?"

"Actually, I should be getting home, I have someone I have to call," Sarain responded, thinking of Eddie getting off shift soon; she had much to tell him.

"It's pretty late for phone calls, but far be it from me to suddenly start acting like your father," Aion replied with a grin. He began to get up from his seat when Sarain quickly said, "How can I reach you? In case I want to see you again."

Aion's eyes lit up and he smiled again, "I'm staying in this little hole in the wall inn on the edge of town. I can't promise that I'll be there to receive your call, but you can leave me a message with the desk clerk."

He gave Sarain the number of the motel; the place was called The Lazy Days Inn, and it sounded like the name fit the place. There was apparently no real maid service, since no one had come to clean his room for the entire stay. The television didn't work, and Aion was sure that something else was leaving in his room since he was constantly finding little droplets of "evidence" on the floor. But the place was cheap, and no one asked questions about the hours he kept or what he did for a living. Sarain too gave Aion her number, but made no mention of where she lived; she would save that for another time when she felt more comfortable with him.

When they stood up and said their farewells, a silent second went by, neither knew what the proper thing was to do in their situation, and neither felt ready for hugging. Instead, Aion extended out his hand to her, and Sarain shook it goodbye. They left the bar separately, like strangers, and headed their separate ways. As Sarain walked away, she peered over her shoulder to see Aion doing the same. He smiled at the coincidence, but she didn't return the smile, she merely watched him for a moment then turned back around.

The man was still a stranger to her, and not at all what she had imagined him to be. Demon hunters to her had always been stern and emotionless men like her grandfather. The only exception was Orran who had only been a boy, and Eddie if you could classify him as a serious hunter; she considered him more of a part-time trainee. Aion though seemed like a normal guy, maybe a personality more of a bounty hunter than a demon hunter, she didn't think such a thing was possible. Surely a life hunting evil beasts would bring the cynic out in a person, like it had Sarain, but Aion still had hopes and emotions.

As Sarain trekked home she began to wonder if perhaps it wasn't the work she did that led her to her pessimistic lifestyle, but her life itself; the choices she had made, and the ones that had been made for her. Sarain had a long way home to think it over, and it was nearly three when she approached her home.

Sarain suddenly slowed her approach when she saw the figure of a man waiting outside her door. It couldn't be Eddie, since they had previously agreed on an earlier occasion that he would not make surprise visits to her place, and they usually would go to his place anyways. Sarain wasn't expecting anyone; she wasn't the type to have visitors.

The night was dark as the clouds covered the moon and she regretted not having put in a light outside her door; a light would certainly help the situation, because it would allow Sarain to see her unexpected visitor.

Sarain reached for her waist and suddenly remembered that she was unarmed. Though since she couldn't avoid her home, she had nothing left to do, but approach the man with caution. She just hoped this was a friendly visitor and not one looking for a score to settle.

Chapter 9

As Sarain drew near her steps alerted the man of her presence, and he quickly turned around to see who was approaching, and in that moment Sarain recognized her visitor, and felt a wave of relief come over her. It was James. His face too looked relieved as she approached him. He appeared to have cleaned himself up since the last time she had seen him, but his expression was still solemn.

"Why are you here?" Sarain asked him.

"When you didn't show downtown, I figured I'd come to you," he answered her.

"Actually I did go to meet you, I was just running late," she explained.

"Oh, I was wondering where you were," James commented, as he sat down on the steps leading to her door.

"Have you been waiting long?" she asked curiously, gazing down at him.

"A while," he answered, but gave no actual detail to how long.

They were silent for a moment. Sarain knew she couldn't invite James in, the barrier in her door frame wouldn't allow him to enter, and his tired posture already making itself at ease on her steps, told her that he had no intention of going in anyways. So Sarain sat down next to James on the steps, staring out into the darkness of the cloudy night, waiting for him to say something to break the silence.

Finally he spoke by saying, "Do you really think we could stop them?"

"Cyrus and Desmina? If we can find them, I can stop them," Sarain told him.

"They're stronger than you realize," he muttered.

"Maybe, but you don't know how strong I am," she told him in return.

"You can't take them on when their together, you'll have to get them when they're apart," James warned.

"Didn't you tell me that they were virtually inseparable?" She asked.

"Yes, but Cyrus does have his taste for beautiful women; it's a habit Desmina could never break him of and she doesn't accompany him when he's feeding that desire," James explained.

"You think I could use myself as bait? I don't know what Cyrus prefers," Sarain remarked.

James turned and looked at Sarain, having him suddenly staring at her while so close made Sarain uncomfortable, it reminded her too much of another vil sang, one she rarely let herself think of.

He must have seen the discomfort on her face, because James quickly looked away, and then replied, "It'll work; you're definitely his type."

It became silent once more, this time awkwardly so, and it was Sarain who decided to break it by saying, "It's getting near dawn... You should probably go."

James nodded, and began to stand up, but then Sarain suddenly stopped him to say, "This time don't disappear for so long. We're really going to do this... Stop them that is, but I need your help to do so," she nearly pleaded with him. Sarain didn't want to see James give up, and still worried that he might be on the edge. She felt as though his fate was in her hands, and it wasn't a responsibility she wanted to have, but she couldn't so easily clean her hands of him either.

James looked down at her like he wanted to say something, but then simply gave her a smile and a nod before leaving. The whole interaction seemed so normal as though they were two friends having a conversation, but it was the casualness of it all that made it feel so weird to Sarain, and she almost had to remind herself that James was still a vil sang.

Sarain stood up and finally headed inside her house. She thought of calling Eddie, and telling him about the many events that had unfolded throughout the day; it was late, but it wasn't a strange hour for her to call, he should be just barely getting off work.

Sarain went into her bedroom, and without a second thought collapsed onto the bed and then grabbed her phone. The whole act made her feel like a schoolgirl excited about calling her boyfriend, except the excitement wasn't there; instead it had been replaced with the disturbing feeling of someone watching her. She put the phone back down, then turned around and found the eyes that were watching her.

Delmar's reflection hovered in the mirror again, he watched her quietly as though unseen, but his image was clear to her. A sullen expression was on his face, and his once stern dark eyes now looked weak and helpless.

"Why are you here?" Sarain grumbled to him.

He didn't answer right away, his eyes simply followed her, and his stare was beginning to infuriate her until Sarain realized that he wasn't giving her a judgmental glare, but instead a look that showed his own shame.

"What do you want?" she asked him, with significantly less harshness in her tone.

"I wish I could have been a better grandfather to you," he weakly spoke.

"We can't change our pasts; we have to live with the decisions we make. I think you told me that once," Sarain replied emotionlessly.

"Even so, I was still the only family you had, and I was never really there for you," Delmar stated with sorrow.

"That doesn't matter now... Besides, you are not the only family I have," Sarain relayed to a perplexed Delmar, "I met my father tonight."

A sudden look of bewilderment came over Delmar's face and then his soft expression was gone and an enraged one emerged. His voice turned fierce and the grandfather she had always known became very visible in him again when he spoke, "Stay away from that man, he will only bring you trouble!"

"What? How dare you! You have no right to tell me to stay away from him; it's because of you that I never knew him before now!" Sarain shouted in defense.

"Your father is not the man you think he is," Delmar yelled back.

"You were never the man you should have been!" Sarain blurted out. Delmar then suddenly hesitated, hurt by Sarain's word, and before he could respond Sarain quickly said, "I am not the helpless child you tormented, and you can't do a thing to hurt me now! You are dead, and you should stay that way!"

Sarain suddenly grabbed the mirror, lifting it off the wall, and shoved it with Delmar's stunned reflection staring back at her into the back of her closet, the mirror facing the wall. She then slammed the door closed, and stormed out of her bedroom.

It was true, Delmar could do nothing to her now, but still his words cut through her. The only difference was Sarain now had the power to walk away. She wasn't going to let a ghost stop her from knowing the father she never had. She just hoped her grandfather wasn't speaking the truth.

Sarain woke up on the couch, hours later, to a peacefully quiet house. Light filled the room with the sun shining through her windows. She looked to a clock hanging on her wall and noticed that it was nearly noon. She didn't feel quite rested enough, but she didn't want to go back to sleep. All she could think of was Eddie; it felt like ages since she had last seen him even though it had only been a couple days, but so much had happened that she needed to tell him. She felt like she was going crazy. Eddie was an open-minded guy, but even he would question her on the things she had seen as of late. Though still she had to tell him, she had to talk to someone about it; she was so tired of keeping everything inside.

Sarain got up, and went into her bedroom. The mirror was still in the closet where she had left; she noticed as she grabbed herself fresh clothes, but she didn't dare to touch it. She wasn't the least bit curious in seeing if Delmar was still there. She closed the closet door when she was done, and quickly headed out to see Eddie.

It was a bright warm day out, barely a cloud in the sky. Birds were chirping and a small group of kids were playing in a park nearby. It was a beautiful day, but it was something Sarain wasn't used to seeing. She spent so much of her time tracking and hunting at night, that she usually slept her days away. Her skin had become pale, and her eyes were not used to the brightness of the day, and after a little while of walking in the heat, she started to regret picking the dark clothing that she had.

Sarain remembered once being a child and playing in the sun, but the memories were a blur, and had been buried under many years of forced training followed by even more years of survival. She couldn't remember if she had been as happy as the kids she saw outside as she walked and passed them by, but she hoped she had been. She had little these days that did make her happy, but Eddie was one of the few.

About halfway on her trek to his home, she realized that she should have called him first before leaving to make sure he would even be home. He didn't work too many day shifts, and rarely went out anywhere socially. In fact, since meeting Sarain, Eddie had pretty much lost all his social ties he once had; after learning of the darker side of life, things never quite looked the same to him again. Sarain was his only real tie between the world as he had known it and the darkness that he had discovered, being both his girlfriend and his guide.

Sarain hoped that he would answer as she arrived at Eddie's door. She rang the bell of his condo, and waited for him to answer. She stood there for a minute, listening for someone stirring inside. Silence. She rang the bell a second time and waited again. Still no answer.

Sarain began to walk back down the steps from Eddie's door when she heard his door creak open behind her. She turned around to see a sleepy eyed Eddie staring down at her.

"You're here early," he groaned and stretched.

"It's after noon already," she replied with a smile.

"That's normally early for even you," he whined, but then smiled back.

"Are you going to invite me in?" she asked, waiting for him to step aside so she could get by.

"By all means," he answered, moving back and pulling the door open further.

Sarain slinked up the stairs, and walked inside with Eddie closing the door behind her. Eddie was shirtless and still in his pajama pants; it was obvious that she had woken him. He walked to his kitchen and poured himself a glass of water, then turned to her and asked, "Did you want anything?"

"No," she replied while shaking her head.

Eddie took a long drink from his glass before placing it back down and finally saying, "So were you missing me or something? It's not like you to just show up like this, especially during the day."

Sarain's eyes looked away as she stated, "I needed someone to talk to."

Eddie's eyes widen and he replied, "You never need to talk; this must be good then."

Her eyes met with his and she said with a tone, "I'm serious... I met my father last night."

Eddie's smile went away and his expression looked concern when he asked, "Really? Did he even know about you?"

"No," she answered.

He looked confused and questioned, "Wait, how did you even find him? How do you really know he's your father?"

"There are not a whole lot of middle-aged guys walking around with purple eyes. Besides, he knew my mother," she stated.

"Wow," Eddie simply said. He walked over to Sarain and put his arms around her; he kissed her on the neck, and whispered to her, "Are you alright?"

Sarain closed her eyes and said, "There's more."

"Well, tell me then," he replied softly.

"I saw my…" Sarain started to say, about to tell Eddie about her grandfather, but then found herself hesitating. She worried that he would think she was crazy, and she really didn't know how to tell him anyway. She barely believed it herself and she had seen so many strange things. She couldn't tell him, and instead found herself saying, "I saw… James… he was pretty messed up the other day."

"Well I would think so," Eddie stated, still holding onto Sarain.

"He was a little better last night when he came over to talk about finding Cyrus and Desmina," Sarain started to go on when suddenly Eddie let go of her. She looked up at him to see a strange look on his face; he then asked her, "He comes over to your place?"

Sarain stared at him with confusion and responded, "Well he did last night," she paused wondering why Eddie seemed worried and then continued by saying, "It's not like he can come inside, the barriers are still there."

Eddie brushed a hand through his hair awkwardly and said, "I know, but he's still a vil sang."

Sarain nearly laughed, "It's not like I don't know how to take care of myself."

"Yeah but…" Eddie began to say when Sarain realized why he was acting so strangely.

"Wait, are you jealous or something?" she said almost appalled.

Eddie backed away while shrugging awkwardly and saying, "N…No, come on, I'm just worried about you."

"Oh my god! You are jealous," Sarain said raising her voice.

Eddie just looked at her, not defending himself or giving an explanation before he finally said, "Well it's not like he's a bad looking guy."

Sarain rolled her eyes and said, "I can't believe this, it's so ridiculous!" She then turned and headed for the door.

"Where are you going?" Eddie asked trying to stop her.

"Home, I don't need this," Sarain stated. She opened up the door and started to step out when he called out, "Come on, don't leave."

But Sarain had already heard enough, she had never given Eddie a reason not to believe in her faithfulness and the idea that she would hook up with a vil sang of all people just made the situation that much more insulting. Sarain had never told Eddie about Winston and now knew that she never would; she felt he would only use the knowledge to further feed his suspicions.

The trek home went by a lot faster, and the day no longer felt so sweet. Sarain came home just as frustrated as she had left it, this time with no way to let it out. Then she thought of Aion staying at the Lazy Days Inn, and wondered if she should call him. He was at least one man that Eddie couldn't be jealous of her spending time with. Delmar may have warned her about him, but then he too had always been too judgmental and overprotective of her as well.

Sarain wondered if her father would wind up falling into this category one day too.

Chapter 10

By early dusk Sarain was once again meeting with her father at the same bar they had sat down in the night before. This time they sat in a booth near the front window, both watching as the sun hit that bright pocket of orange before finally setting. The sky was many shades of pink and blue, it was beautiful like many sunsets were, but what made it feel extra special was the fact that it was the first one Sarain could actually remember watching with a parent. She wasn't normally the type of person to get caught up in such sentimental things, but even she felt the aura that this was a special moment. They both watched quietly as the sun set and when it did, Aion turned back to her and said, "It's amazing."

"The sunset really is beautiful," Sarain commented.

"Yes, but what I was trying to say was that it's amazing that I have such a wonderful daughter," he remarked while staring at her.

"You don't know me that well yet," she stated.

"Maybe so, but I'm not blind. You're just as stunning as your mother, maybe even more so," he said with a smile.

Sarain gave an awkward smile, she wasn't used to being complimented, and had not been compared to her mother in a very long time. Her mother had always been known as the fairest member of her clan, and as a child Sarain felt like she could never compare next to her mother's beauty. Even after her mother had passed away, she had felt that the memory of her beauty would always overshadow any possibility of her own.

The booth's bench seats, while cushioned, were still hard and worn, and as Sarain shuffled to adjust to her seat, hoping to make it more comfortable, she felt her necklace swing out from where she kept it hidden under her blouse. It caught Aion's attention and he recognized it quickly.

"That's your mother's ankh, isn't it?" he remarked.

"Yes it is," she replied surprised.

"Wow, she used to wear that every day, well at least when I had known her," Aion said reminiscing.

Sarain smiled and replied, "Yeah, she still did up until she gave it to me." Aion smiled in returned and they were quiet for a moment. Then Sarain looked at him with a question in her mind and asked, "How did you meet my mother?"

Aion's expression changed, and he almost looked sad, his eyes looked to the window as he began to say, "I helped her clan when they had needed the aid of a hunter who was knowledgeable of the area that I happened to be from. They had been apparently looking for some kind of mythical beast that was supposedly in the area. They were there for a while searching for this thing. It was in that time that I courted Ariana. When they began hitting dead ends on their search, it was then that I am ashamed to say that I gave them false leads in hopes of keeping Ariana and her clan there longer. I imagine it was when her father, Delmar, finally realized what I had done and why, that they suddenly took off so urgently. I had tried to talk her into staying with me not long before then, but she never gave me an answer. I had assumed when she left with them that it was on her own accord, but I have had doubts about that since then."

Sarain sighed, realizing that in his story he gave an explanation as to why Delmar had warned her about him. He had caught him lying to their clan, and it was no wonder why he didn't trust him. But the fact that Delmar had warned her at all, completely disregarding her need to know her father, only made her detest for her grandfather grow. As Sarain was thinking of this, another part of Aion's story stood out to her and she had to ask, "What was this mythical beast they were looking for?"

"I'm not sure," Aion said while trying to rack his brain, "It was one of those almost fairytale like creatures, I think it was called an Ancient, or something like that."

Sarain froze up when she heard that name; it was the same creature that had popped up in the hunter's guide she had found. The same kind of beast that the author and even she suspected may have been behind the attack on her clan. If her clan had been hunting and searching for it even back then, then perhaps her grandfather really did find it. There was a reason after all that no one was able to give a description of the creature if no one ever lived to talk about it. She herself had never seen it, but now more than ever she needed to know more about it.

Sarain looked to Aion, but the look on his face told her that he knew nothing of the creature. He had already more than once referred to it as a work of fantasy. It was obvious that he didn't believe in the creature and knew little about it, maybe even less than what was stated in the hunter's guide. He would be of no help to her.

Aion took notice of the vacancy on his daughter's face, and lowered his face down till he made eye contact with her. He gave her a soft smile and asked, "Are you thinking of your mother?"

"A little bit," Sarain replied, and it was true, her mother was on her mind, but there was also so much more.

Aion sat up straight and then lowered his eyes once more as he asked, "How did she die?"

Sarain gazed up at him with a feeling so surreal, she never imagined talking to anyone about her mother, and especially with anyone who had actually known her. Looking at her father's face, she could see the sadness in his eyes. He must have truly loved her mother. By the look on his face he still did, but now it would be a love that could never be returned.

The memory of her mother's death still felt strange to Sarain, almost as if it had been a dream and that her mother had never truly existed. Sarain couldn't see how hearing of her mother's death could help Aion any, but if he wanted to hear it then she would start from the beginning, "Let's see, first she got headaches and would tired easily. Then she started having these dizzy spells. She tried to hide it at first, until she collapsed one day. It was then when our doctor told her that she would need lots of bed rest. We all thought it was a temporary thing, like a bad flu, and that it would eventually get better and go away... But it didn't. She got sicker, and started throwing up. And then she was always in bed after that. My grandfather restricted her visitors; he was afraid that someone would carry germs to her that could make her worse. Even I wasn't allowed to see her... The illness was long and slow, but at the same time it almost felt fast, you know," Sarain's eyes began to well up as she remembered her mother, and she said, "It's strange, I can never remember my mother being sick before then, not even so much as a paper-cut. Even the people around her always seemed healthy, but after she got sick, it was like the whole clan became vulnerable; people started getting colds and flus, the elderly got arthritis, women had miscarriages. It was like a plague, and things were never the same after she died."

Aion stared sorrowfully at his daughter and said, "Your mother was a very special lady, even when I knew her you could see the way the rest of the clan looked up to her with their faces full of respect and adoration. It felt like it was about something more than just her being the chief's daughter."

"I noticed that too," Sarain remarked, recalling.

"Did they look at you the same way?" he asked her.

"No, I could never live up to their high standards for me. I wasn't my mother," she replied with a bitter tone.

Aion gazed at her then asked, "Was Delmar one of these people?"

She returned his gaze, a little surprised that he had figured out her grandfather so well in the short time he had known him. She stared at him for a moment before finally answering, "Yes, he was one of many."

Aion then shook his head in frustration and said, "I'm so sorry you had to go through that. I wish I could have been the one to raise you."

Sarain forced a smile saying, "I know..." But Aion stopped her there; he quickly took her hand and looked her in the eye with his expression serious, and stated, "No, really, if I had known about you I would have stopped at nothing to find you."

Sarain held her breath, caught off guard by the intensity that her father spoke. She had never in her life believed that anyone would care about her so greatly. Aion was nearly a stranger to her still, but just knowing that they shared the same blood was enough for him to love her. Sarain didn't know what to do with that. She couldn't say that she honestly loved him yet, but she did respect him. One thing she could say was she was glad to have finally found her father.

Sarain parted ways with her father, the night was still early enough to hunt, and Sarain wasn't ready to go home. She had debated inviting Aion along, the idea of hunting with another experienced fighter did seem appealing, but the urge to be alone was greater. Besides, Sarain always preferred to hunt solo; she found it easier to not have to worry about another person: if they were okay, where they were standing, or if they might get in the way. There was always a liability to hunting with someone, and Sarain was still learning how to deal with working with others.

The streets were noisy at this time of night; busy with traffic, both cars and pedestrians. Everyone was out having a good time, making plenty of targets for demons to feed upon. But the busy streets also meant that it would be harder for a creature to go unnoticed.

Sarain kept a watchful eye on everything that moved around her, but nothing appeared out of the ordinary. Not even a pale face in the bunch. Sarain trotted along the sidewalk, she walked a while before finally deciding to give up the hunt. She looked around and found herself in a familiar setting; she had hunted near this place before, and it was usually quite active. She was at a park; it came complete with a jungle gym and a sandbox. There was also a pathway and benches, colorful trees and bushes, and even a basketball court. The park was rather large and usually busy, but that night it was much calmer, just a small group of teenagers hovering around the swings.

Sarain sat down on a bench, and began to watch the teenagers. They joked around with one another, horsing around and laughing. There were four of them; two boys and two girls. They looked young, perhaps freshmen or sophomores in high school. Sarain couldn't help but think of Kit as she watched them; he would have been about their age. She wondered how much his looks would have changed, how tall he would have been. Would he have been taller than her? She'd never get to know the kind of man he would have been, and she wondered about that every day. She had failed Kit, and the memory of him never left her mind. She would close her eyes and see the image of his body lying motionless in the darkness. His eyes would be vacant and glassy, his neck would be broken, and no breath would escape his lips. Sarain sometimes worried that she was forgetting his face. While his memory haunted her, the details of his appearance were beginning to blur. She couldn't remember what shade of brown his eyes were; whether they were so dark that they were nearly black or light like they were almost hazel. She couldn't remember his voice at all. It nearly killed her how much it hurt, knowing that it was her fault that he died, and here she was forgetting him.

Sarain looked away from the teens, and cast her eyes to the ground, but she couldn't bear to close them. Not again, not with knowing that his image would flash before her once more. Her eyes began to burn, and she knew that she couldn't avoid it. She closed her eyes to blink, but took more than a moment to open them. A tear escaped her eye. She watched as the teenagers left the park, and sat there alone in the dimly lit night, still thinking to herself. The night was growing later and the air was getting cold and still Sarain sat lost in thought.

It wasn't until the crackle of leaves crunching that caused Sarain to jump up to her feet. She quickly spun around ready to fight, but stopped herself when she saw a familiar face: Eddie. She put her machete down, and walked slowly to him.

"What are you doing here, Edward?" Sarain asked with a serious expression.

Eddie sighed and said, "I know you usually hunt around here, so I came looking for you... I wanted to apologize, for earlier."

"You mean for being a paranoid ass?" she commented.

"Basically, and a stupid jerk too... Do you forgive me?" Eddie spoke giving her a soft smile.

Sarain could see the sincerity in his eyes. Eddie loved her, and it was that same love that made him get irrational, but he never meant to hurt her. She didn't think he was even capable of it.

Sarain returned his smile and said, "Of course I forgive you."

Eddie quickly approached her, and wrapped his arms around Sarain. He kissed her on her forehead, and closed his eyes as he said, "You don't know how much you mean to me."

Sarain looked up at him curiously and asked, "How much is that exactly?"

Eddie opened his eyes and turned his head down to look at her, and spoke with a serious expression on his face, "If anything ever happened to you, I don't think I could live."

It was something no one had ever said to Sarain, and she believed him. But she wasn't sure if it was something she was happy to hear; it left an uneasy feeling in the pit of her stomach.

Chapter 11

Sarain dropped her sword and grabbed at her stomach; the pain was making it too heavy to lift. She dry heaved from the pain, but the act of her stomach muscles clenching just made the pain worse. She felt the weight of her body start to tip her over, and as her knees began to buckle forward, she found a strong arm suddenly wrapping around her chest to keep her from falling.

She felt too weak to move and merely directed her eyes up instead of moving her head to see who had caught her. She immediately saw Orran's hazel eyes looking down at her with worry. He held her still as she leaned in his arms, still trying to catch her breath.

"I'm so sorry I left you with him," he said to her.

Sarain panted for a moment longer, and choked out the words, "It's not your fault."

Orran still shook his head and said, "I saw what he did; if I hadn't have walked away, I could have stopped him."

Sarain struggled to look up into Orran's eyes while she told him, "When my grandfather makes up his mind to do something, nothing can stop him… He wanted to teach me a lesson; even you wouldn't have been able to stop him from doing so."

"Maybe, but that wouldn't have stopped me from trying," Orran told her.

"And you probably would have ended up on the ground next to me," she remarked.

"No, the chief wouldn't have gone so easily on me," he commented.

"You call that easy?" Sarain asked with surprise.

"I could see that he was holding back. You are his granddaughter after all, but I am nothing to him. I would only be a disobedient peon to him. I'd be lucky if he left me alive," he said to her quietly.

Sarain gazed up at Orran in amazement and asked, "Do you really think he would be capable of murdering one of his own clan members?"

"I wouldn't put anything past that man," he replied.

What he was saying could get him in a lot of trouble if anyone else heard him, but Sarain believed what he said. Delmar had the will to do anything he set his mind to; she just wasn't sure what kind of thoughts clouded his mind. But the look on Orran's face told her that he had a better inkling of what those thoughts were, still she couldn't bring herself to ask. They stayed there in silence for a minute longer until Orran finally asked, "Do you think you're good to walk?"

"Let me see," Sarain spoke unsure. Orran helped her stand up straight and the moment his hands left her back, Sarain began to stumble, and he caught her once again.

"I guess not," she said sounding exhausted.

Orran gazed down at her and said, "That's okay," then lifted her up into his arms, and held her close to him, "I'll carry you wherever you need to go."

Sarain clung on to him, and asked, "How long are you willing to do this?"

"As long as you need me," he answered.

But Sarain couldn't bring herself to say what she wanted to tell him: I'll need you forever.

Sarain shot up in bed, and it took her a moment to remember where she was. She lay safely in her bed, alone. Eddie had tried to get her to let him stay the night, but she never felt right with having another body next to her while she slept. It left her feeling too open, too helpless.

Sarain's memories always came to her so clearly in her dreams, just like the mirrors reflected her nightmares so easily. Things she would have thought had been long since forgotten would suddenly come rushing back to her once she would close her eyes to sleep, making it impossible for anything to truly ever be forgotten.

The dream of her memory felt so fresh, that Sarain could almost swear that she could still feel the warmth of where Orran's hands had been on her. She could still smell him, but that was impossible. The dream had only triggered the memory of him in her senses; he had been dead for ten years. He had promised to be there for her as long as she needed him, but he failed to keep his promise; she needed him still, but he was gone.

Sarain clung to her bed sheets, holding back tears, and wondering why she still longed for a man who had been gone for such a large portion of her life. They never even got to be more than just friends, and yet he left such a void in her heart. Maybe it was meeting her father that was stirring her past up, but it seemed as of late that she was living more in her past than in her present, and she wasn't sure why.

Was it seeing Delmar in the black mirror? Why... why couldn't she see Orran, or her mother, or Kit? Why did it have to be her grandfather?

Then she thought to herself; all the dreams, all the memories, were related to Delmar in some way. He always made an appearance or was referred to. Perhaps he was the reason for all her flashbacks, but was he behind them or just the trigger? That man...Sarain had always tried to find reasons why he had treated her the way he did growing up, but understood now that there was no good reason. Even Orran had seen through him those many years ago, but he wasn't the first. No, someone else had grown a dislike for him long before either her or Orran lost faith in him. And that person was Ariana, her mother. She had almost forgotten how much the two of them had fought.

They would argue in hushed tones, and every time that Ariana would raise her voice to Delmar, he would make her be quiet.

How could Sarain have forgotten? She played as a small child, pretending to be oblivious to it, but she knew they were fighting, but never about what; whether it was the same thing, or just many little things. She just knew that it was often, and that it didn't stop until her mother became ill, then Delmar became the devoting father and ever overprotective. That's how she had mostly remembered him with her mother, but that wasn't how it was.

Had she repressed these memories or just simply forgotten them until now? It was like a key had unlocked her brain and lost memories were becoming found. Still, there was something important she was missing. Where in her memory did it lie?

Sarain laid back in hopes to dream again, but her dreams would give away no more visions that night, only restless sleep.

Sarain sat on the steps to her house early the next evening, waiting for James to arrive. He had called her not long before to let her know that he had found information on Cyrus and Desmina, and would stop by to debrief her on this information. Sarain had tried calling Eddie to let him know, given how he reacted to their last meeting, and wanted to invite him to come so he too could be debriefed, but she could only get his voicemail. So she left him a message letting him know what was happening, and hoped that he wouldn't act like the jealous type again.

Sarain sat there watching the clouds move over the moon; sometimes it would be bright, and other times it would be dark from being mostly hidden. The air had a chill to it that night, and a constant light breeze. Sarain tucked her hair behind her ear to keep it from blowing into her face. She was dressed comfortably, all in black, and all covered up; it was how she normally dressed. She didn't like to wear anything too tight or revealing, or even too brightly colored; she didn't want to draw any unwanted attention to herself and she needed clothes that she could easily move and fight in.

Sarain looked up when she heard approaching footsteps on concrete nearby. She saw James walking towards her carrying a brown paper bag under his arm. She didn't bother to get up to greet him; it wasn't like they were friends after all, this was about business. Sarain just gazed up at James as he neared, and when he reached her she made room for him to sit down.

After a moment went by for him to settle, she turned to him and asked, "What did you find out?"

"They've been seen hunting together in a rundown neighborhood on the edge of town. They've even been stealing other vil sangs kills," James told her, "They're getting sloppy."

"They sound like animals," Sarain stated.

"They are animals," he remarked.

She turned and looked him in the eye and asked, "And what makes you so much different from them?"

James looked a little surprised by the question, but quickly answered in defense, "Because I haven't lost my humanity."

Sarain stared at him for a moment longer, and then turned away and said, "Good... I meant no ill will by the question; I just wanted you to remember what we are dealing with."

"I remember every day when I think of what they did to my children," he stated.

"I know, but you also have to remember that if all you seek is vengeance, you too will lose your humanity and will become just like them," she said, "It doesn't matter if you have demon blood in you or not; that kind of hatred engulfs all."

"Are you speaking from experience?" James asked her with a look upon his face.

"I'm speaking as someone who doesn't want to see you lose your way... Besides, I would hate to have to kill you one day," Sarain replied. James turned to her, half expecting for her to smile after having said a joke, but there was no smile upon her face, only a solemn glare. She wasn't joking; she would kill him if ever she had to.

James looked away from Sarain, a little annoyed at her lack of faith in him, but at the same time he couldn't blame her. She barely knew him, but did know that he was a demon half-breed, and she was a killer to his kind.

Sarain noticed James' sudden distance from her, and reached out to him. She placed her hand on top of his, and he quickly turned and looked at her with surprise. "I didn't say that, because of the demon in you. I said what I said, because I don't want to see you lose the man in you," she told him reassuringly then she quickly moved her hand away from his.

James continued to stare at Sarain for a moment, until she turned away from him altogether, and then there was an awkward silence. To break the awkwardness, Sarain gazed down at James' paper bag and asked, "What's in the bag?"

"Oh," James almost shouted with sudden remembrance, "It's something I figured you would need." He handed the bag to Sarain, and she slowly unfolded the rolled up top and opening to the brown crumpled bag. She gazed into it with curiosity and then reached in to pull out the contents. The cloth was soft and light with slickness to it. She pulled it out to find herself holding a silky white dress.

Sarain looked at the dress in confusion and asked James, "And why are you giving me this?"

"It's what Cyrus likes... You'll definitely catch his attention in it," he responded.

Sarain held the dress out to get a better look at it and then replied, "Well, who wouldn't, it's not much more than a nightgown."

"Well it'll work better than your usual apparel," James commented.

Sarain glanced down at her clothes and asked, "What's wrong with what I'm wearing?"

"You look grungy," James answered, and then he gave her a smile and asked, "Do you even own a dress?"

"I don't need to impress you," Sarain stated with a serious tone then she smiled back at James, but didn't answer his question. James waited a moment to see if Sarain would add anything else, and when she didn't, he said, "Well, I guess I have my answer."

Sarain turned back to the dress and gave it another glance over. She then said, "I'm not even sure that I can pull off wearing something like this. I'm not really the kind of girl who dresses like that."

"You'll look beautiful," he mumbled.

Sarain glanced over at James to see him staring back at her. She quickly turned her eyes back to the dress and stuffed it back in the bag then said, "Well, hopefully it'll work." She motioned that she was about to get up, but before she could, James was already on his feet and lowering a hand to her to help her up. She took his hand so not to be rude, but was already regretting doing so. James pulled her up causing her to stand close to him. He stared down at her and Sarain looked up into his green eyes, his gaze so intently set on her. She wanted to move away, but didn't. Sarain simply watched as he watched her trying to read what he was thinking; looking over his expression. She had seen this look on the face of a vil sang once before, and knew that it could only mean trouble for her. Yet still she didn't look away.

James began to slowly lean in towards Sarain, but she did not lean in return, and he noticed this and stopped. He continued to gaze down at her and didn't break eye contact until the sound of footsteps approaching them echoed out.

Sarain then closed her eyes and thought to herself, how perfect and horrible his timing was. She didn't want to open her eyes to see an angry Eddie, but feared she soon would.

Chapter 12

Sarain gazed over to see who was approaching her and James, and suddenly became relieved to see that it wasn't Eddie. It was Aion, and then she immediately realized that she had never told him where exactly she lived, and was curious to how he had found her. She quickly backed away from James, and turned to her father and asked, "What are you doing here?"

"Well, hello to you too," Aion said a bit amused.

Sarain shook her head for a second, realizing her manners, and then said, "Sorry, I'm just surprised to see you."

"Yes? Well I was surprised how easy you were to find… Do you really think hiding in plain sight is a good idea?" Aion remarked. He then glanced over at James and gave him a curious look. Sarain took notice to this and turned to James and said, "James, this is Aion… my father."

"Oh," James immediately said then he held out his hand to Aion, and added, "It's a pleasure to meet you." But Aion merely stared at James and made no motion to shake his hand. Finally James lowered his hand back to his side and said in an apprehensive tone, "Okay… I should be going anyway."

James turned to Sarain and gave her a forced smile then proceeded to go down her steps. He avoided Aion's stare as he passed him by, and once he was out of range, Aion turned to Sarain and asked, "You do know what that man is right?"

"Yes," Sarain said a little surprised to how honed her father's hunting skills were, "I know he is a vil sang, but he's also a good informant."

"Really?" Aion said with some confusion, "Well he sounds like someone who doesn't know how to be loyal to any side."

Sarain gave her father a curious look and asked him, "Are you doing the protective father routine on me?"

"Well what am I supposed to do? I am your father, and I plan to protect you," Aion remarked.

"I am capable of protecting myself, you know," Sarain replied.

"Hey, watching over you is my god given right," Aion said to her with a smile.

Sarain smiled back and nearly laughed, it was funny to her that she would suddenly have a stereotypical father, demon hunting aside. Sarain then turned and opened her door while saying, "It's a bit cold out here," and then walked inside.

Aion followed, but then stopped short at the doorway and looked up at the frame. Sarain spun around and stared at her father for a moment and asked, "What is it?"

"Nothing," he said slowly, "I just noticed that you use the same barriers as your clan." She glanced at him curiously and asked, "How did you know? I hid the barrier."

"I can smell the sage," Aion remarked.

"Is it really that potent?" Sarain asked.

"Yes, very much so," he replied then stepped past her to get inside. Sarain closed the door behind him, remarking, "I guess I must be used to the smell."

They sat down in Sarain's den, and were silent for a while until Aion finally thought to ask, "So what exactly has this James been helping you with?"

"Well, there's this demonic vil sang couple in town that he has been helping me track," she explained.

"Have you killed them yet?" he asked curiously.

"No, I have to get them separated first; they're too strong together," she replied.

"Do you need help?" Aion asked with a hint of a worried tone.

"No, I have plenty of help... Really, I don't think it'll be that difficult," Sarain told him reassuringly.

"Sounds like I have a strong daughter," he stated.

Sarain gave her father a slight smile, she wasn't sure what to do in this situation, she still wasn't used to having a father and she also wasn't used to entertaining guests. She gazed over at Aion and asked, "Did you want a tour of the place?"

"Sure," he replied a little uncertain of how to interact as well.

Sarain got up and led Aion throughout her small home, guiding him from room to room. The tour was quick and short, and ended with her showing him her bedroom. There she went to her closet and pulled out her small safe hidden in the back. She opened it up and pulled out her photos, and handed them to Aion.

"I thought maybe you might want to see my mother," Sarain told him.

Aion slowly shuffled through the pictures until he found the one of Sarain and Ariana. She only had the one, her clan didn't really keep cameras around and only took pictures when they were around towns and dealing with people who kept cameras. He stared at the photo intently, and appeared lost in thought.

"I was about three there," Sarain remarked referring to the picture.

Aion continued to stare down at the picture, silently. A good long moment went by before he finally spoke, saying, "Your mother really was beautiful." He then traced a finger over the photo and said, "So this is my family... Or at least it was."

Sarain could see the sorrow on Aion's face as he gazed at the life that he missed out on. He looked at her mother's image with so much love in his eyes; she would have thought that his feelings for her would have faded with time. But as he stared down at the picture in his hands, it was as though not a day had gone by, and he was still a young man in love with a girl.

Aion finally broke his gaze away from the photo and handed it back to Sarain. She put the photos back into the small safe and placed it in the back of her closet. As she closed her closet door, the black mirror caught her eye. She finished closing the door, and turned to her father and asked, "I have a kind of odd question for you."

Aion gave her an inquisitive look and said, "Okay… Go ahead and ask me."

"Do you see anything strange in mirrors? … What I mean is, is there anything that isn't supposed to be there?" she muttered while looking towards the ground trying to avoid her father's troubled eyes.

Aion was stunned by the question and quickly asked Sarain, "No. Why? Do you?"

She avoided the question by asking another, "Do you know if my mother did?"

Aion shook his head, "I really wouldn't know that… Perhaps it is something your clan could do; they were quite advanced and well-trained people."

"Yeah, maybe," Sarain mumbled unsure, and a little worried about letting her father know too much about her.

Aion continued to stare at his daughter with concern and asked her, "Is there anything else like this that you can do?"

She hesitated answering her father, but felt that she could trust him, so she decided to tell him what he wanted to know, "I seem to be a little stronger than most people..."

"How much stronger?" he questioned with an uneasy tone.

"I can kill a demon with my bare hands, or at least I have on more than one occasion," Sarain answered sheepishly.

"Well, adrenaline can make us do strange things... Is there anything else?" Aion asked.

"I heal faster than other people," she replied.

"Okay. That you got from your mother... She was a healer you know," her father explained.

"I do remember something like that; it's why everyone treated her like she was precious," Sarain commented.

"Well, she was a kind pure-hearted person as well," he stated reminiscing.

Sarain gave her father a moment, and then started again by saying, "So nothing with mirrors and you? ... Not even black mirrors?"

"... Black mirrors? Well those are different, people have been using black mirrors to communicate with the dead for centuries, but it has to be an authentic one, not something a person can purchase at some trendy little mall shop," Aion remarked, "Why? Do you have one?"

Sarain began to answer her father and then for some reason found herself saying, "No, I just heard something about them." She wasn't sure why she said it, but the lie was out of her mouth before she could think twice.

Suddenly a knock came to the front door, and Sarain went quickly to answer it with Aion following behind her. It was getting late, and she was surprised by the prospect of having yet another visitor in the same night. She turned the knob and opened the door to see Eddie standing on the other side.

He immediately reached for Sarain and gave her a slightly sloppy kiss, and then said, "Sorry it took me so long, I didn't get your message till after my shift ended."

Eddie tried to kiss her again, but this time Sarain managed to stop him. She pushed him away, and stepped aside so that he could see Aion in the room. Eddie's eyes immediately went to the man standing nearby and he quickly said with a tone, "Who's this?"

"'This' is my father, Aion," Sarain replied shooting Eddie a dirty look, she then turned to her father and spoke; "This is my friend, Edward."

"You kiss all your friends?" Aion observed.

"No, just this one," Sarain answered feeling a bit nervous.

Eddie suddenly got a slightly panicked expression on his face, and he approached Aion saying, "Sorry about that," and stuck his hand out to shake Aion's, "Sarain told me that she found you."

Aion gave Eddie a fake looking smile, but didn't shake his hand, instead he stepped past him and towards the door, saying, "I really should be going, it's late."

Eddie fake smiled back at him and said while trying to ignore his actions, "It was nice meeting you." But Aion didn't reply and just stepped outside.

Sarain watched as her father went down the steps, and then closed the door behind him. She turned to Eddie with a scowl upon her face. He simply laughed, and said sarcastically, "Well that went well."

Chapter 13

"Are you sure you don't want my help?" Eddie asked with concern.

"I don't think I'll need it," Sarain called out from her bedroom, "Besides, James will be nearby if anything goes wrong."

"Great," he sarcastically muttered under his breath as he waited for Sarain to come out of her room. "Are you okay in there?" he asked curiously.

"Yes, just trying to figure out the lacing on this thing," she replied.

Eddie laughed then hollered back, "You can hunt better than anyone I know, kill hundreds of demons, but you don't know how to put on a dress?"

"Quiet, I almost have it," she shouted back.

"This should be interesting," he mumbled to himself. Then his eyes went to the doorway of Sarain's bedroom as her door slowly opened. His mouth dropped open and he sat there staring at her in awe as she stepped out in her white dress.

Sarain looked over at Eddie with an unsure expression on her face and asked, "Do I look alright, not too weird or anything?"

Eddie continued to stare at her for a while before answering, and when he did he stammered, "You...you look incredible."

Sarain gave him a funny look and said, "I couldn't possibly, I feel completely out of my element in this thing, but I guess it'll have to do."

Eddie quickly got up as Sarain walked into the room, and stated, "I would feel so much better if you let me go with you and James for this. I promise I'll stay back with him when you're actually trying to lure out Cyrus. I just want to be there in case something happens."

"I told you, I'll be fine," Sarain insisted.

"Yes, you said that, but I would still like to go," he continued to press.

She gazed over at him and asked, "This isn't a jealousy thing, is it?"

Eddie sighed in frustration and replied, "No, it isn't. It's an 'I want to protect my girlfriend' kind of thing."

Sarain smiled at Eddie and took him by the hand and stated, "Don't worry so much, I'll be alright." Then she looked down at her dress with confusion and asked, "But where do you think I should put my weapon?"

The moon shone down brightly as Sarain slowly walked down a deserted narrow alley. Her steps echoed loudly on the stone beneath her feet, making it very easy for herself to be heard. The buildings were tall and made of brick on either side of her, and the alley stretched far; there would be nowhere for her to run or hide. But she would never flee; she wanted to be found, that was why she had come there.

Sarain slowed her pace until she finally stopped walking altogether. There was no demon hunting her, or at least that she could tell. She was where James had told her to go, while he waited in a building across the street. He had wanted to stay near her in case she needed backup, but Sarain worried that Cyrus would catch his scent and realize something was wrong. And maybe he did, for Cyrus was nowhere to be found. He and Desmina were supposed to be squatting in one of the many abandoned buildings in the area, and Sarain could probably track them to it with time, but that would still put the couple together and stronger. If Sarain ever hoped to stop them she needed to get them separately, and now might be her only chance. If she continued walking these streets night after night her scent would linger and become familiar, and the demons could become suspicious.

Sarain stared up at the sky. The night was full of stars and the sky was cloudless. The moon was still half hidden in the shadow of the earth, but its light shined down on her. The air carried a chill that blew Sarain's hair back and off her shoulders, and made the fabric of her dress sway in the wind.

It was the middle of the late night hours, and Sarain had been walking the slummy streets for some time to no avail. She was surprised that she hadn't run into a regular demon or vil sang, or even an ordinary criminal at this point, just by pure chance and likelihood. And this made her think, that perhaps these streets had already been over swept by two demonic vil sangs, who could have already taken out the everyday street garbage, and chased out any weaker demons. They might have moved on by now to a richer and fresher killing ground.

The air was quiet, so quiet, that the only sound Sarain could hear was her own breathing. This mission was a waste, Sarain thought to herself, she had let James down. It looked like Cyrus and Desmina had already gotten away, once again.

Sarain sighed and decided to call it quits. She turned and headed back towards the building she had left James in. She hurried her steps as she grew colder. She saw the building she needed to reach within her view when a strange shuffling sound echoed in her ears. It was faint, but Sarain was sure of what she heard. She turned and looked around, but nothing could be seen in front or behind her. The air was quiet again, but now she was sure something was near her; she could feel the cold eyes fixated on her.

Sarain's eyes scanned around her, but still nothing. Then another soft creak echoed out, and she closed her eyes. She had realized her mistake, she had thought that she was the one waiting all this time for Cyrus to show, and thinking she had been waiting alone was her mistake. Cyrus had been there the whole time, watching and waiting for the right time to make his move. He had noticed her right away. She just hadn't seen him; looking down at her.

Sarain reached for the knife strapped to her thigh as quickly as she could once she heard the sound of feet kicking off against brick. Her hand barely wrapped around the hilt by the time Cyrus came crashing down on her.

Sarain was knocked to the ground with incredible force, and her shoulder slammed hard against the stone pavement. The ground was cold and dirty, but she wasn't there long. A pair of strong clawed hands was pulling her up to her feet and she was soon face to face with an enormous beast. He barely even resembled a man anymore; his skin was gray and bumpy, and his eyes glowed a bright lime green.

It took Sarain a moment to grasp that her feet no longer touched the ground; he was holding her up firmly by her shoulders causing further pain to shoot down her arm. Still, he had her at eye level with him, and she realized that Cyrus was extraordinarily tall. He smiled at her with a mouth full of razor sharp teeth, and then he said, "You are such a pretty little thing, you really shouldn't be walking these streets alone."

"And you should be more careful of the women you pick up," Sarain remarked to him right before she furiously kicked him in the stomach causing him to drop her. She fell to the ground hard again, but this time managed to get up on her own.

"You're surprisingly strong, you must be a hunter," Cyrus bellowed out with his deep voice, "But that won't be a problem."

Sarain ripped away the knife strapped to her thigh, and turned it towards Cyrus. She immediately stabbed him in the chest, aiming at his heart. In reflex, Cyrus swatted her back and knocked her to the ground, leaving claw marks across her chest. She then turned and watched as Cyrus pulled the knife out, seeming perfectly unharmed, and then threw the blade a ways away.

"You should have brought a bigger knife," he told her while staring down at Sarain. She watched as he crouched down into the position of a cat, his arms and legs bending in ways that a human's could not. Sarain tried to scramble away, but Cyrus pounced on her before she could get enough distance between them. He smashed her into the ground, and Sarain's head slammed hard against the pavement. She didn't black out, but her vision blurred.

Sarain's body throbbed as Cyrus lifted her into the air. He held her one handed by her waist, and she tried to kick, but found her feet only hitting air. She swung her fists at him, but his arms were so long that hers could not reach him. She knew she had messed up by underestimating her opponent, and the only option she had left was to call out for James, and hope that he could help her, if he could even get to her in time.

Sarain found herself doing what she thought she would never do, she was screaming, it was a sound that was foreign to her. She had heard plenty of screams in her time, but never her own, not like this. She had screamed in pain before, and even in grief, but never in fear, or helplessness. She had exhausted all her defenses, and this was the last thing she had. Her voice echoed out, and maybe it was her possible concussion, but it felt to her like the earth around them was vibrating from the sound of her scream.

Cyrus quickly covered Sarain's mouth with his free hand to silence her, and said, "Now, now, none of that. We can't have people rushing to ruin our fun." Sarain continued to struggle and Cyrus tightened his grip on her waist till she winced from pain. She muffled out a groan from beneath Cyrus' thick hand, and he smiled. He stared at her swinging figure and said, "It looks like I've already been a little rough on you, and I'm just getting started. It's a good thing you're a strong hunter, or this would be over too fast."

Cyrus then pulled Sarain closer to him, his long arms bending inward, and she was now close enough to swing her arms at him. She pounded on him with her fists and kicked him with her feet, but it had no effect on Cyrus. He just laughed and pulled her closer. Sarain could feel her energy draining as exhaustion set in, but she remained fighting and squirming, with her cries still muffled under his hand. Cyrus brought Sarain's face close to his and he stared into her eyes.

Sarain didn't close her eyes, but simply gazed into his. His eyes shone with the fiery demonic blood inside of him. An intense lime green stared back at her, and his eyes reminded her of a jack-o-lantern. It felt to her as though he were trying to hypnotize her with his gaze. Her body was going numb, but it may have been from her being elevated. Her head began to spin, but she was sure she had a concussion. She tried in her mind to fight him off, and not to let him in.

When Cyrus finally decided that Sarain was weak enough and had no fight left in her, he uncovered her mouth and took her by the throat. He brought his mouth to her neck, and when Sarain felt his icy cold breath against her skin she shivered and muttered a soft, "No."

"Still have a little fight left in you, I see. Don't worry. I don't plan to kill you…yet. I just want a little taste first before I have my fun with you," Cyrus whispered in her ear with his hoarse voice.

She felt his lips on the skin of her neck, and they felt like ice. He was much colder than other demons she had fought; he wasn't room temperature, not even slightly cold, but instead he was freezing. She could feel his lips pulling back and his teeth dragging against her skin. Sarain shuttered, and Cyrus groaned as if pleased by the quiver of her body. Then the searing pain set in as his teeth broke through her skin. Blood flowed from her neck and into his mouth, and the only thing Sarain could think of was the color of Kit's eyes; cherry wood.

Sarain could feel herself fading, and her eyes grew heavy. But before she could close them, Cyrus suddenly threw her down, and spat out her blood. He wiped his mouth in disgust, and Sarain stared up at him with blurry vision. Blood stained her white dress and glistened on the silky fabric. Sarain struggled to get up, but remained limp. She watched as Cyrus slowly stepped towards her, staring down at her in confusion.

"What are you?" he said glaring down at her, "Because that definitely didn't taste human."

Sarain stared up in disbelief: Had she heard him correctly? Was she not human?

Chapter 14

Cyrus continued to glare down at Sarain, "Answer me," he demanded, but Sarain couldn't. She didn't have an answer for him, and wasn't sure she was even able to speak. He bent down, and picked her up once more, and gave her a better glance over. His eyes studied her image, and he said, "How is this even possible?" He then took a better hold of her and threw her onto his shoulder to carry, and stated, "I'm taking you to the Ancient, he'll know what you are."

As Cyrus turned and began to walk off with Sarain, her eyes caught a glimpse of the image of someone running at them, and she mustered up the strength to call out his name, "James."

He leapt and tackled Cyrus from behind. Sarain went tumbling to the ground, and before long she was struggling to get to her feet. She looked to Cyrus to see James already on him and stabbing him with his blade. She stumbled as she rose, and felt a pair of strong arms catch her. Sarain gazed up to see Eddie holding on to her, he had come anyway, and most likely had found James, and had been waiting with him.

Eddie picked Sarain up and carried her to a safe distance before sitting her down and racing back to help James. Sarain laid there weakly as she heard the roaring animalistic screams coming from Cyrus while James and Eddie continuously stabbed him to death, hacking away at his limps and insides. The horrific sound went on for what felt like forever to Sarain before finally there was silence once more.

She laid waiting for Eddie to return, and when he did, James followed close behind him. Both men were covered in dark demon blood, and both looked relieved to see Sarain. James had a large claw mark across his chest, much like her own, but his looked deeper and larger, still he walked without a limp. Eddie's clothes were torn and dirty, but he appeared unharmed, James had taken the brunt of the beating in this fight.

Eddie crouched down by Sarain's side, examining her injuries, and then looked to her face and asked, "Are you okay to walk?"

Sarain tried to nod, and began to get up, but quickly collapsed into Eddie's arms. He picked her up, and carried her down the block to where he had parked his car. "It's a good thing I'm not all about walking everywhere like you," he said trying to lighten the mood.

Sarain tried to smile at him, but could no longer hold her head up. She passed out as James helped Eddie place her in his car. The last thing she could remember seeing was the concerned look in both men's eyes.

Sarain opened her eyes. The room was dimly lit, but she recognized it as her room. She laid snug in her bed with her wounds freshly dressed, and her clothing changed into less binding and more comfortable attire. She looked around, barely moving her head, and realized that Eddie was lying next to her on the bed, but he wasn't asleep. His eyes were open and he was watching her intently. He sat up once he saw that she was awake and said, "You're awake. I was worried, I thought you might have a concussion, but when I saw how quickly your chest wounds were healing, I figured you'd be alright."

"My wounds?" she said weakly.

"The claw marks you got along your collarbone, they've already sealed up. I'd give them less than a week before they're gone. You heal so fast," Eddie said with amazement.

It was then that Sarain remembered the events of that night, and what Cyrus had said about her not tasting human. She did heal fast, incredibly fast, too fast, and all because of a mother who healed people. Sarain had never before questioned her mother's power, but now she wondered where that power came from, and why a demon was so disgusted by her blood. Then Sarain remembered something else, Cyrus had mentioned the Ancient, and taking her to him, that meant that the creature had to be nearby, perhaps somewhere in town.

Sarain shot up in bed and was suddenly hit with a wave of pain. Eddie flinched up when he noticed this and stated, "It's way too soon for you to be doing that!"

"The Ancient, we got to find it," Sarain muttered incoherently.

"The what? Whatever it is can wait," he insisted.

Sarain looked around the room, things were still hazy to her, and she asked, "Where's James? What happened to him?"

A look came over Eddie's face and he said, "He went home, he can't come in, remember?"

"Oh," she mumbled, and sagged back into the bed. Eddie covered her back up and remarked, "You need to stay covered, you're still cold. You lost a lot of blood."

He then looked at her neck wound, which was bandaged up, and stated, "This one is healing a little slower, but I think it will be okay." He looked at Sarain with concern and asked, "How'd you let yourself get bit?"

Sarain groaned and started to say, "I...I didn't let myself get bit..."

"Hey, never mind. Don't worry about it, he was stronger than we all thought," Eddie quickly said when he noticed that Sarain was straining herself to talk, but she started again by saying, "You came."

Eddie smiled down at her and nodded saying, "Yeah, I came. I wasn't about to leave you on your own, whether you needed me or not."

Sarain looked up at Eddie with tired eyes. He sighed and kissed her on her forehead and said, "Go back to sleep, you need your rest."

Sarain's heavy eyes complied and she shut them once more. She felt like she had so much to tell Eddie, but hadn't the strength to do so. She was grateful for his care and devotion, even if she couldn't tell him so. And Eddie simply watched as Sarain slept, thankful that he still had her within his grasp.

Sarain woke up in the afternoon of the next day feeling well rested and with a lot more strength. The room was bright with light, and she lay in bed alone. She strained herself a little to get up, but was surprised how well she was able to move on her own. Her waist and shoulder were sore from the trauma they had taken, but her neck hurt most of all, and Cyrus had only taken a small taste. She couldn't imagine the pain that people went through when demons ripped out their throats the way they usually did, but then again, those victims usually died quickly. Her neck ached and the muscles along it felt strained and sore throughout and down into her shoulder blade. She felt crooked and didn't want to move her head, but her chest felt fine. Sarain was curious about the claw mark she had received to it; it had been bad enough to get blood all over the front of the dress she had worn, but she could no longer feel the pain.

Sarain pulled down at the neck of her loose fitting shirt, and looked for her wound. She saw a bandage with dried blood taped to her chest. She peeled it back at the corner and could feel the dry blood pulling away with the gauze. It felt like someone ripping off a band-aid, and was worse the slower she went, but when she was done, her breath caught in her throat. The wound was completely healed. There wasn't even a scar. Even with her fast healing, it should have taken a week, but the wound had healed overnight.

The bedroom door creaked behind Sarain, and she quickly pressed the bandage back on, and then turned around to see Eddie standing in the doorway.

"You're still here," she said with surprise.

"I called in with a family emergency. I figured you would need my help today," Eddie explained, "But it looks like you're moving around fine." He moved towards her, gazing at her curiously and asked, "How are your injuries?"

Sarain placed a hand over her chest bandage and quickly said, "Still sore." She didn't know how to tell him the truth, which was that her injuries were miraculously healing fast, because she might not be human.

"Well that's to be expected," Eddie replied. He approached Sarain with the look like he wanted to hug her, but he didn't knowing the pain she must be in. He smiled at her and said, "You realize that that was the first time I've ever stayed the whole night at your place. You've never let me do that before."

"Well I was kind of passed out and all," Sarain remarked.

He smirked and said, "Either way, I liked waking up to you next to me."

Sarain gave him a weak smile in return, and Eddie didn't notice her lack of enthusiasm. She knew where he was going with this and wasn't ready to discuss it, but he was still headed there anyway.

"What do you think about us moving in together?" he said with Sarain hoping that he wouldn't.

Sarain rubbed her forehead and replied, "I think you still have a lot of time on your lease, and my place is a better location for what I do."

"I could take the hit for breaking my lease, it's really not that big of a deal," Eddie remarked.

"Yeah, but our schedules often conflict with one another; one of us would be moving around while the other is trying to sleep," Sarain responded.

"I could learn to get used to it," Eddie stated, starting to notice her hesitance.

"Well, creatures are often coming around here looking for me, and I wouldn't want them finding you instead," Sarain said with a little harshness in her tone.

"Your place has a barrier on it, and I can take care of myself. I think I proved that last night when I saved your ass," Eddie spoke, starting to snap back.

"With James' help," Sarain shot back, raising her voice.

"Yeah, with James' help," he mocked back at her, "Your precious James!"

"What's that supposed to mean?" she demanded.

"You called out his name, and not mine," Eddie whined.

"I saw him first! I didn't even realize you were there at the time," Sarain explained.

"Yeah, because you didn't want me there!" he shouted at her.

Sarain let out a heavy sigh and began to say, "Damn it Win…" and then quickly stopped herself, and covered her tracks by saying, "When are you going to drop this?" Her heart started to race once she realized her mistake. She had started to say 'his' name and it was a name she never let herself say. Eddie didn't seem to notice, and why would he, he knew nothing about 'him'.

"Drop what? Drop the fact that you clearly seem too comfortable with James, or drop the fact that you don't want to live with me?" Eddie angrily commented.

Sarain turned to Eddie and stared into his eyes, and stated, "This is the last time I'm going to tell you this, you need to stop worrying about James. The only reason I didn't want you coming was because I didn't want to risk you getting hurt. And it's crap like this that makes me think that we aren't ready to move in together."

Eddie got quiet, and they both went silent. The tension turned into awkwardness, and Eddie finally said, "I'm sorry. I was totally wrong. I didn't mean to…" But Sarain cut him off by saying, "You never mean to, but that doesn't stop you."

Eddie stopped talking and looked at Sarain with sadness in his eyes. It was the same puppy dog look he always gave her after they had an argument, and she would usually forgive him, but not this time.

Sarain stared up at him, and worked up the courage to say, "I think you should leave."

Eddie nodded reluctantly and immediately left the room, and it wasn't long before she heard her outer door shut behind him as well. Sarain felt horrible, but she couldn't fight with him anymore, or at least not at this moment. She couldn't go on pretending that everything was the same and normal, not after what had happened last night. Her life as she had known it had been suddenly ripped away from her, and Eddie was acting like it was just another Tuesday. It wasn't his fault really, he couldn't possibly have known, and Sarain didn't want him to. She feared that he wouldn't look at her the same.

How could he, when she herself didn't know what to think, because really, what was she?

Chapter 15

Sarain sat on the edge of her bed and raked her mind for a thought or a clue to why her blood would be different from other humans. Her mother was a healer, but Sarain didn't know how or where her power came from. Sarain knew that over the years she had grown stronger and healed faster than the year before, and could never explain why. She didn't know what she was or how she was, but simply that she was.

Then she thought of the pounding headache she had had weeks ago, and the ungodly piercing pain that ravaged her head. And she wondered if her blood would taste different if she were dying. Perhaps her power and her mother's power came with a price. Her mother had died at her age, and maybe she was dying now.

Sarain groaned with frustration; she had to know. She needed to know why. She just didn't know where to begin to look for the answers. Then she was hit with another revelation, the mirror. Her grandfather, he was the only link to her mother, and he might know how this all was possible.

Sarain went to her closet and retrieved the black mirror. She looked into its darkness, and saw no image, but her own. She shook it, unsure of how exactly it worked, but nothing happened.

"Work!" she yelled at the object, but still nothing. She gripped the frame tightly, and screamed into the mirror, "Delmar! Delmar, show yourself!" She waited for some kind of action, staring intensely at the mirror, but nothing changed. "Damn it, show yourself already!" she screamed once more, and Sarain shook the mirror furiously.

Now that she finally wanted to talk to her grandfather, he was nowhere to be found. It felt like a sick game; everything. The pieces of the puzzle were finally falling into place, but still there were no answers. The Ancient was likely in town, but now Sarain worried that she wouldn't live long enough to find and question the beast.

The anticipation was too much for her to take. She needed answers before it was too late, but couldn't find the path in which to start. She sat down on the corner of her bed with the mirror on her lap, and stared into the darkened glass. She looked at her reflection and wondered if anything would change; would her hair fall out, would her eyes sink into her skull? Her mother's looks changed before she died, Sarain wondered if hers would do the same. Aside from the one excruciating migraine, Sarain didn't feel like she was dying. She was in fact healing faster than ever. If she were dying wouldn't she be getting worse?

Sarain continued to stare down at the mirror, still hoping and waiting for something to happen. She gazed at her violet eyes, to some they seemed strange, but they looked normal to Sarain, and in the shadows they almost looked brown, like her mother's.

She closed her eyes, thinking; what am I doing? Nothing was wrong with her, except for the fact that she was taking the word of a demon, one that had tried to kill her even. She took a deep breath and then exhaled slowly. Silence.

Plop... plop. The unexpected soft noise caused Sarain to open her eyes. She looked down at the mirror to see two droplets of blood staining the glass. She stared at it confused for a moment before she realized that her reflection showed that the blood was coming from her nose. She reached up to wipe her nose when a sudden and intense wave of pain went surging through her body. Her whole body stiffened and immediately pulsated, and her limbs began to thrash.

Sarain lost control of herself and started convulsing on the bed. She felt the mirror slide off her lap, and couldn't stop it from dropping. She shook violently as her head grew hot with a high pitch squeal ringing through her ears. Her eyes throbbed painfully, and her jaw ached from clenching her teeth. Her hands were balled up into fists and she could feel her nails digging into her skin. Her heart pounded so hard that it felt like it was going to rip out of her chest.

Sarain panted heavily and prayed for the pain to stop, but in the middle of trying to focus on making the pain go away, Sarain had the revelation to stop praying. Whatever was happening to her, and if she was dying, prayer would do nothing to stop it. She had prayed for many things over the years, but the tragedies kept coming. The only thing that ever made a difference was her, and her ability to fight her way through whatever mess she found herself in, and that was what she would do again. And if she couldn't fight this, if there was nothing she could do then she would live her life as she always had until there was no breath left inside her. But she would not pray to god again.

It was about an hour before the pain subsided. Sarain finally cleaned the blood from her face, and removed the bandage from her chest; there was no point in hiding a missing wound when there was no one around to hide it from.

Sarain walked over to the mirror that laid face down on the floor, and hoped that it was still intact. She bent down and lifted the mirror up then slowly turned it around. A long crack stretched across the glass, and Sarain nearly choked up when she saw it. The mirror was broken, not completely, but she feared that it no longer harnessed the power to summon spirits.

Her eyes nearly welled up, but she couldn't fully understand why. She knew she wanted answers, but it was the thought of never being able to talk to her grandfather again that was bothering her. She hated him, but he was the only link to her past, the only family from the life she had once had. It was true that she had her father now, he was living and breathing, and he was her blood, but Aion was never a part of her past. He was an acquaintance, barely a friend, and he did not feel like family.

Sarain placed the mirror back into her closet; she wasn't willing to part with it, and she was hoping that it still may work. She walked to her bathroom and turned on the faucet at her sink. She let the cold water run then splashed it on her face. She took a washcloth and wiped away the dried sweat off her body. Sarain then looked at her hands to see them covered with dried blood and half-moon scars being the source of it. The blood was also caked under her nails, and she made sure to clean them well. The scars weren't bad, and would probably heal before anyone would see them, but Sarain felt the urge to cover them up. She felt ashamed that they were there at all, and she didn't want them seen, but a part of her was also ashamed to hide them. She felt as though she was hiding a lot these days.

Sarain shut off the faucet just in time to hear a knock against her door. She quickly toweled off her face, and went to see who was visiting at this hour. She wondered if it could be Eddie wanting to apologize to her again. She reached for the door knob and turned it open. There stood James waiting on the other side.

Sarain was a little surprised to see him, and at the same time not surprised at all. She stood there in her doorway, knowing that James couldn't come in and asked him, "Why are you here?" He glanced at her nervously, caught off guard by her questioning of him, and answered, "I just wanted to see if you were okay."

Sarain quickly glanced over herself, and replied, "It looks like I'm fine… Is that it?" James didn't answer right away; he couldn't understand why she was being crude. He finally muttered, "I guess so," and turned to walk away when Sarain abruptly stopped him by saying, "Wait, I'm sorry about that. I'm just a little on guard right now."

James sighed and gave her a slight smile, and said, "It's alright. It's understandable after last night. I'm just surprised you're moving around so well." "Well, you seem to be doing okay yourself. I saw that you got pretty banged up," Sarain observed.

"Yeah, but I'm a fast healer, it comes with the whole being half demon," he remarked, "What's your excuse?" "Fast healing runs in the family," she replied, then stepped outside and closed the door behind her. They sat down on her steps like they had done before, and Sarain suddenly remembered Eddie accusing her of being too comfortable with James, and she started to wonder if he was right.

James gazed at Sarain who was looking distant and asked her with concern, "Are you sure everything is alright?" She turned to him and forced out a weak smile, but said nothing in response.

He looked away and gazed up at the sky. They sat in silence for a while until Sarain turned to James and asked, "Are you okay?"

He smiled softly, "I think so. It's just strange." "What is?" she asked curiously. "Cyrus being gone... He helped turn me, and after my children... well... I just thought vengeance would feel better," he explained to her.

"I get that... You build up something so much in your mind, that when it finally happens, you're still left feeling empty and unfulfilled," she remarked. "Vengeance especially, never leaves you feeling quite the way you think it will. It's like it almost makes it worse, because afterwards you realize that there is no peace at the end."

"Sounds like you know a lot about it," James took notice. Sarain looked up at him and said, "I do."

"That's too bad," he commented then turned and stared out into the night. Sarain watched him; she studied his profile, and wondered about the man he once was. "What were you like when you were human?" she found herself asking him.

James turned back to her, caught off guard by the question, and answered, "I was just a guy... I had been married briefly, had my kids when I was young. When I got divorced I got a little lost," he gazed down as he continued; "It was Desmina who found me while trying to make Cyrus jealous. She turned me, and tried to make me her pet."

"How old were you?" Sarain asked.

"I was thirty at the time, it's only been a couple of years since then, but it feels like forever," he replied.

Sarain wondered and had to ask him, "Did you want to become a vil sang?"

"I didn't know what I wanted; change or maybe for everything to just stop. My life was spiraling out of control at the time," James answered.

"And what about now, does your life still feel that way?" she questioned him.

James gazed down at Sarain, staring into her eyes, and said truthfully, "It did, but things are beginning to get clearer." She watched him for a moment, and when he didn't look away, she did. She then stretched and rubbed her sore shoulder. James took noticed and asked, "Still hurts?"

Sarain smiled, thinking how she still wasn't healing as fast as she would like even with her abilities, and answered, "Of course."

"Yeah me too," James replied, placing a hand on his chest over his wound, "I guess I'm not pulling off the macho demon man act very well."

"You're doing fine," Sarain joked, and then she remembered how he looked in the blurry moments that she saw him in the night before, and said, "You really took a beating, didn't you?"

"Cyrus wasn't a weak demon," James remarked, but Sarain was beginning to realize more. "You saved me," she said remembering more clearly.

"Eddie and I both did," he said humbly. Still something else was standing out to her; Eddie barely had a scratch on him, but James had been mauled up, and then she realized, "You protected Eddie, didn't you?"

James turned his head away from hers, and gazed away. He didn't answer for a long while, but when he did he spoke softly saying, "I thought it was what you would have wanted."

"Why do you care what I want?" she asked with a little defense in her voice. James immediately turned and stared at Sarain as though the answer was obvious, but he didn't say anything in response.

The air had suddenly changed and Sarain no longer felt comfortable, she stood up quickly and put her hand on her door, and then said to James without turning around to see him off, "Let's give it a few days for us all to heal up, and when we have, well go after Desmina."

"And after that?" James asked with a longing curiosity.

"After that our business is done," she remarked, and then opened the door and stepped inside. She slammed the door close before James could say another word. She couldn't have this conversation; she couldn't do this again.

Chapter 16

Sarain stood in the center of a deserted crossroads, nothing but wind could be heard, and only dirt and mountains could be seen for miles. She stood there cold, her clothing torn and mostly missing, she clung to what little fabric she had left hoping that it wouldn't blow away in the wind. Her hair fluttered in the breeze dancing freely, and though she was nearly naked, it was the exposure of her neck that left Sarain feeling helpless. She couldn't see them, but she knew that monsters were waiting, lurking until the sun would go down.

Sarain was alone with the sun beating down on her back, but its light gave her body no warmth. The wind grew stronger, and she tightly wrapped her arms around herself for coverage. Clouds rolled in fast, and Sarain looked up at the sky. Dark clouds were approaching and it looked as though a storm would soon be there. The breeze brought a chill to her spine, and she knew that something much more troubling was coming than the storm. Something bigger than her average battles. She just hoped she would be strong enough to see it to the end.

Daylight was disappearing behind the black clouds and the shrieking of monsters began to echo out from the shadows. With nothing in sight, Sarain didn't know where to turn, and the sky was growing darker. She began to crouch down with fear, hoping that hiding her face would save her, for if they couldn't see who she really was then perhaps they would leave her be. Sarain closed her eyes and remained as still as she possibly could as the screeching grew louder. She waited for her inevitable horrific end, but it was the feeling of warmth on her neck that caused her to soften from her tensed position.

"Hey lady, what are you doing down there?" a familiar voice called out.

Sarain slowly gazed up with hope in her eyes, and saw a friendly face staring down at her. "Edward," she whispered. He gave her a smile, he was standing in the only remaining sunlight, and he said to her, "How many times have I asked you to call me Eddie; only my mother calls me Edward."

She started to stretch up as she answered, "But that's not your name."

Eddie lifted his head up slightly as an animalistic shriek rang out, and then turned his attention back to Sarain and held out his hand, saying, "We should leave, they'll be here shortly."

Sarain stared at his hand and wanted to go with him, but couldn't bring herself to take his hand. "No, you can't protect me. They will come regardless."

His smile faded, and he stood back, taking his hand away from her reach. Eddie gazed down at her with disappointment and spoke coldly, "Yes, they will come, and I won't be here forever, but do you really think that he can protect you better?"

Eddie's eyes then focused on something behind her, and Sarain quickly spun around to follow his gaze. "James," she muttered softly. His green eyes brighten from the sight of her. He smiled at her, and began to extend his hand out to her as well.

"You know I'd do anything to protect you," James called out to her. Sarain watched him curiously as he waited for her to reach out for him, and she began to bring her hand up when she realized that James was surrounded by darkness, and that the light that shone down on him was moonlight, not day.

She stopped her hand, but James continued to smile and wait patiently for her. Sarain's heart began to ache; this was too hard, and she couldn't see her path. And as if reading her mind, a voice echoed out, "That's because you need light to see your way."

Sarain turned around once again to see the brightness of a new dawn behind her, and standing in that light was another man, Orran. He looked upon her with strength in his posture and love in his eyes. She smiled at him upon recognition, and he returned her loving gesture.

"You've been waiting for me, haven't you?" Orran spoke softly to her.

"Always," she answered from the depths of her heart. Sarain reached for Orran as he extended a hand out slowly to her, but she couldn't quite touch him.

"I'm close, just a little further," he whispered to her. She leaned out for him, but he seemed to grow farther away. The more she reached the further Orran got. Eventually Sarain realized that he was leaving her and she cried out, "Don't go! Don't leave me here alone…" Her voice cracked and weakened as she pleaded, "Please… Take me with you."

But he continued to fade away, and Sarain quickly leapt out to reach him. She leapt into the darkness he had left behind, and fell to her knees with no one to catch her. Orran was gone, and he had left her alone; James and Eddie had also disappeared, and only the shrieks of distant demons remained.

Sarain began to cry and felt cold as ice while lying on the ground waiting for it all to end. She knew it was her fault, but she didn't want to be all alone. And as she wiped her eyes, she spied a glimmer of light from the corner of her view. She raised her head and saw the dim orange glow of a sun setting. The colors were beautiful, and though this meant that darkness was soon coming, the sight was still stunning to Sarain. And standing in this fading light was a figure. Sarain knew who he was without having to approach him for a better look. He haunted many of her dreams, and his name never escaped her lips.

"Winston," she muttered faintly. He was where she had left him; so far away. He gazed up at her, and she realized that he had heard her speak. She had barely even whispered his name, but he heard her calling out to him. He had no smile for her on his face, and his eyes held no hope. Winston did not reach out for her, nor did he take any steps towards her. Instead, he simply watched her from afar, standing perfectly still.

Sarain raised her head up further and began to pick herself up as Winston gazed on. As she stood up on both feet and dusted herself off, she no longer felt cold or fearful. She then stared back at Winston, and over the distance she whispered to him, "Are you waiting for me?"

He watched her, but didn't answer. Sarain stood there waiting for something, anything, to happen, but nothing did. They stood there in a stalemate, until Sarain finally mustered up the nerve to make the first move. It wasn't a step forward, or a gesture of kindness; no, instead she glared at him, and called out accusingly, "It was not my fault..." Her voice weakened with a slight pinch of guilt and she whispered, "I never asked for you..."

Sarain shot up in bed, and it took her a moment to realize that she had only been dreaming, and was not on trial. The room was still dark, it was not quite day yet, but soon would be. She placed her hand on her pillow to readjust it for more sleep, but found that it was drenched. At first she figured she had been sweating from her intense dream, but then realized that the room as well as her body was cool.

Sarain pondered for only a moment before she slowly reached her hand up to her face and touched her skin. Her cheeks were damp, and she realized that she had been crying. She quickly shook her head and thought to herself, "No, I will not feel guilty." But she wasn't sure if it was guilt that she had been feeling. If her dream told her anything it was that the only man she truly wanted to be with she could not have.

The realization began to overwhelm Sarain, and emotions came rushing at her causing her to have to fight back the tears. She bit down on her lip wondering why she kept longing for men who were no longer around. She had to constantly remind herself every day that Orran was gone, and also was secretly trying to forgive herself for everything that had unfolded between her and Winston; she felt guilty for having ever slept with a vil sang, but then also felt bad for having left the man.

It had been years since this had all taken place. Sarain had thought she had put that past behind her, but now it all still felt just as fresh as the day after. Why couldn't she let it go?

Why were both men haunting her so?

Two days later Sarain found herself sitting with Eddie at his apartment. They waited for James, whom they were expecting to arrive at any minute to debrief them on Desmina's whereabouts. They thought it best to not discuss the issue in public, but James could not enter Sarain's home so they decided Eddie's was the next best thing.

There was an uncomfortable quietness between Sarain and Eddie. He tried to act as though all was fine between the two of them, but they never resolved their issues from their fight. And every time Sarain looked at him, she thought of her dream, and how she didn't feel at home with Eddie. He was a good man, and she did truly care for him, but there was something off about their relationship; something felt false that she couldn't quite pinpoint.

Eddie stared at Sarain from across the room, waiting for her to say something, anything, to him. He had been waiting patiently, but was growing tired of this act, and finally decided to say, "Are we going to talk about what happened?"

Sarain sighed and then glanced up at him, "There's nothing to talk about… I already gave you my reasons, and you apologized. What more do we have to say?"

"I don't know, but I can tell that things aren't right," Eddie replied with concern.

"When are things ever right? Look at what we do for a living, and tell me, really, how can things be right," she stated.

Eddie sighed in frustration then looked over at Sarain, and asked her, "Why are you even with me?"

Sarain rolled her eyes and shook her head, "I'm with you, because I want to be. Why does there always have to be some greater purpose behind everything with you? Some things just are."

"But you still want to be with me... Right?" he asked with a tinge of worry in his voice. She turned and gazed at Eddie, he looked like a sad little boy, and she was finding it hard to stay mad at him. "Of course I do," Sarain answered him. Eddie smiled at her and got up from his seat across the room. He walked over to Sarain, and just as he reached out for her a knock came rapping on the door. She looked to the door, and quickly got up to answer it, brushing past Eddie. She didn't see the look of disappointment on his face.

Sarain opened the door, and James stood waiting on the other side. "Sorry it took me so long to find the place," he spoke while stepping in, "Your directions were a little off," he said to Eddie. Eddie didn't respond, but his expression changed to one of annoyance that Sarain noticed right away. She closed the door behind James and followed him into the living room where they all sat down, with no one sitting near one another.

Sarain looked up to see Eddie glaring at James, so much so that James too appeared to notice and he sat awkwardly in his seat trying not to make eye contact with him. Sarain cleared her throat to grab the men's attention, and then quickly followed by asking James, "So what have you found out?"

"Oh," he muttered suddenly remembering why he was there and said, "Desmina is held up in a warehouse downtown. She obviously knows something has happened to Cyrus, because the two are never apart from each other this long. I don't think she knows exactly what happened, but still, she won't stay put for long. She'll move to a different territory for safety, which means she'll probably leave town."

"Then we should act soon. We should hit her tonight," Sarain responded to both men's surprise.

"Are you sure about that?" Eddie asked with concern, "You're still healing from our last fight with one of these pair... Besides, don't you want to get your father to help us with this one? He is a hunter after all."

Sarain gazed at Eddie, she didn't want to tell him that she had already healed from their last battle, because if she did it would only bring up further questions, and she had already heard more than enough out of him. "I'm doing much better, and I'm sure I'll be fine," she replied, not exactly lying. "Anyways, I'll have the both of you with me this time," she added.

"And what of Aion?" Eddie continued to question. Sarain sighed and gave him a shrug, "I've already been trying to get a hold of him, but he hasn't returned any of the messages I've left him... I don't think he's staying at the same motel anymore, and we can't wait on him, not with Desmina ready to flee at a moment's notice."

"I agree, we should do this tonight," James chimed in. Eddie then turned and glared at him, and said, "Of course you would, you're the reason we're in this mess."

Sarain immediately turned to Eddie and scolded him by saying, "That doesn't matter. I would have done this either way, they murder children. And I think that takes priority over anything else." She gave him a glare hoping that he would realize that she knew he was still acting jealous, while James sat across from her oblivious to the situation. James could tell Eddie wasn't fond of him, but the reason why was unclear to him; the fact that he was a vil sang took more precedence over his mind than the fact that Eddie could be jealous of him as a man.

"So how do you want to do this?" James asked breaking the awkward silence. Sarain glanced at him and replied, "We'll hit her hard and fast; all of us at once, and she won't be able to react quickly enough to stop us all."

"That doesn't sound entirely safe," Eddie quickly pointed out. Sarain turned back to him and remarked, "Fighting demons is never safe, but if we move too slowly, she'll find an opening and take it. The quicker we move the better."

"And what if you get hurt again?" Eddie said to her with a crudeness to his tone. This time Sarain didn't bother to look at him when she answered, "Then you leave me behind and continue fighting… That's what I plan to do with either of you."

Eddie's expression turned to one of shock, but James was not surprised. Afterwards, Sarain got up from her seat to ready herself with weapons; this time she would be well armed with her favorite machete. James followed after her to do the same, but Eddie sat there in disbelief, realizing that he didn't really know the woman that he was in love with. Sarain on the other hand knew Eddie well or at least well enough to know that she wasn't in love.

Chapter 17

The night was cool and calm, the air was quiet, and all felt peaceful. The stars were out and shining brightly, glistening for all to see. It was nights like this one that made it hard to believe that something so cruel and sinister could be out hunting the innocent.

Sarain silently made her way through the alley and towards the building James pointed her to, with both men following closely. James was the nearest, helping direct Sarain where to go, and though he knew the way the best, Sarain still led the group. Eddie didn't argue with her or James throughout their journey, but it was his silence that bothered Sarain more, because he was never a man to keep his emotions in.

They stepped lightly as they neared the crumbling building, so as not to alert the demon inside. The ground was wet from an earlier shower, making it harder for them to not make noise.

As they approached the door, they found its frame busted from when someone must have broken in. It wasn't a rare sight, but it left the door hanging open, which meant it would be easier to sneak in. They stepped inside making sure to avoid fallen debris, and had to step carefully from then on.

They walked down a narrow hallway until they came to another door, a heavy metal door. Opening it would undoubtedly make a significant amount of noise, but it was the only way forward. Sarain's hand went to the latch, and James helped her steady and lift the door as she swung it open in hopes of making less noise. The door groaned lightly, but the sound did not echo; Sarain hoped it wasn't heard.

The three of them slowly stepped into a large dark room. Boxes and tables cluttered the area, making it hard to see any other objects around. There were no lights and Sarain strained her eyes to see the room around her. She gripped the hilt of her blade tightly, and kept it raised and ready to strike. James glanced around looking for signs of a squatter, but the room was dark even for him. Eddie had moved closer to Sarain, and was keeping a watchful eye on her rather than the room. Sarain still remained in the lead, and took steady steps towards the center of the room.

She walked past a tall pile of boxes, and when she cleared it she saw the sudden flicker of a lit candle in the distance. Its flame didn't provide much light, but its presence proved that someone was staying there, and had been there recently. It was possible that Desmina could have heard the small group entering her dwelling and fled upon that, but Sarain wasn't aware of any other exits, and hoped that the beast was still there, hiding.

Sarain changed directions, and began to investigate on the far side of the room. There were windows that had been boarded up from the outside with some glass panels still hanging in the frame. All the boards appeared to be in place, but Sarain wanted to inspect them more closely to make sure that one of them wasn't really hiding a possible exit for Desmina.

As she approached the windows, one in particular caught her attention. In the glass, the light of the flickering candle reflected making it like a mirror, and in the reflective surface a face stared out at Sarain, but it wasn't Desmina. Sarain knew this face, but not the name of the owner. Many years ago while Sarain herself was just a girl, she came across another girl one day screaming for help. When Sarain came to her aid, she tousled with the beast that was attacking the other girl and in the process had her blade knocked out of her hand. In the time it took her to retrieve her weapon, the demon ripped out the girl's throat, and Sarain remained forever haunted by the memory of her failure.

It was that girl's face reflected in the glass, and it was that night that played out in the glass. Sarain hated her visions, and tried to avoid mirrors as much as possible. As she turned away from the glass, a sudden movement caught her attention from the corner of her eye. It was only a second, but for a moment, the light of the candle had been blocked. Sarain quickly began to turn around, and while she did, she heard Eddie call out, "She's here!" In that moment Sarain felt a heavy hand collide with her face, and it sent her flying back.

She heard Eddie shout her name, and he quickly came running to her aid. Sarain tried to warn him not to, but before she could, the thick body of a beast came running at him and lifted him in mid run, and then threw him towards a wall. Eddie hit with a loud thud, and limply fell to the ground. Before long James was running at this beast as well, his blade already drawn and in mid swing. He swung and missed, then began to swing again, but on the second strike the demon grabbed his arm. The beast squeezed James' arm until he cried out in pain, and dropped his sword. Afterward, the creature hit him in his chest, but it wasn't enough to knock James down, and when the demon realized this it continued to pound on James until it knocked him unconscious.

Sarain regained her footing, and rushed at the beast with her machete pointed forward. She slashed it across the torso, but the blade didn't go in deep. The demon swatted her away once again, knocking her to the ground, and as she tried to get up the demon was on her and lifting her into the air by her throat.

"You are the ones who killed him, aren't you?" the beast demanded in a deep voice. It raised Sarain into the air, her feet left the ground, and she was at eye level to the beast. Like Cyrus, this beast was tall with gray skin and inhuman features, though unlike him, this beast had breasts, and Sarain realized that this creature was Desmina. Only the breasts gave it away as a female, and Sarain understood why Cyrus sought the attention of other women.

As Desmina dangled Sarain in the air, she noticed another similarity to Cyrus, they had the same bright lime green eyes, and both had glared directly into her own. They were definitely demons with kindred spirits, since both had lost the same amount of humanity so much so that their features mimicked one another.

Desmina stared into Sarain's eyes and shouted, "Do you know what you have done? Over three hundred years we've been together." Her grip tightened around Sarain's neck as she said, "You could never even fathom the kind of love that comes with that amount of time..." And as Desmina began to continue, she was suddenly stopped when a flicker of the candle's flame managed to light up Sarain's face a bit more, making her grip around her neck loosened slightly.

Desmina stared at Sarain with sudden realization, and abruptly asked her with a complete change of tone, "Is this about the Ancient?" Sarain's heart felt as though it skipped a beat, this beast knew of the Ancient, but how did it know that she was looking for it?

Desmina shook Sarain, and asked her again after she didn't answer, "Is this about the Ancient?" "It is now," Sarain choked out. Desmina gazed at her curiously and questioned, "Why have you come?"

A moment went by while Sarain contemplated how to answer. She still remained hanging in the monster's grip, and was aware that the beast could snap her neck at any given moment, but her determination to find out more about the legendary demon was greater than her perseverance to stay alive. She heard herself answering, "I've come to learn all you know about the Ancient... I need to know what it is."

Desmina stared at her blankly for a moment, and then began to laugh. Sarain hung there feeling idiotic, but still continued to say, "I know I am in no position to make demands, but even if you kill me, I have to know if this thing is what murdered my people."

"Your people, really?" Desmina asked sounding amused, "I wouldn't know much about that, the Ancient has killed a lot of people, and I as well. I'm sure a number of demons could have killed the people you talk about. But about knowing what it is, well I would imagine you could answer that better than I could."

Sarain felt her body go into a cold sweat, her heart pounded with frustration wondering what this creature could possibly be talking about. She grew angry and with aggravation she said, "Stop playing games; my being a demon hunter doesn't mean I am all knowing about your kind."

The creature laughed again in its deep hoarse voice, and then without notice, threw Sarain down. She collided into the ground hard, cutting her arm open on debris, and nearly knocking the wind out of her, but she still felt able to fight. Desmina continued to laugh and Sarain glared up at her as she reached for her blade.

Desmina stared down at Sarain with no fear of retaliation, and simply said, "If the fact that you're a demon hunter wasn't funny enough, the fact that you're here asking me about the Ancient is hilarious."

Sarain's expression began to change as she grew more annoyed, and now a little curious. She stared up at the demon with her hand tightly gripped around the handle of her blade and asked, "What are you talking about? What makes it so funny?"

Desmina smiled a wicked toothy grin at Sarain and answered, "It's funny, because as its offspring, you should really have a better understanding of it as well as yourself. But then again, since you do kill your own kind, perhaps I'm giving you too much credit."

Sarain's breath caught in her throat, and her body went cold. "You're lying," she shouted at the beast. Desmina continued to stare down at her, unfazed, and Sarain yelled, "How can I possibly be a demon, I've never been infected by demon blood, and I can walk in the sun!"

"I can't explain it either, but being a demon as long as I have I've learned a thing or two about blood, and I can smell from here that your blood isn't human," Desmina stated looking at Sarain's wounded arm.

Sarain searched her mind for an explanation, but knew the beast wasn't lying, there was something wrong with her blood, and Cyrus had tasted it. The strength, the fast healing, even her mother's powers were always left unexplained, perhaps her family's bloodline was rooted in demon's blood. But the question was, that Sarain found herself asking aloud, "Why do you think I'm the Ancient's offspring over anything else's?"

"Well, for one, the Ancient is the only demon I've ever known that can walk in the daylight like yourself, and second, you have his eyes," Desmina relayed to her with a smile on her face.

Sarain's blade fell to the ground.

Chapter 18

"No… You're lying," Sarain muttered under her breath. Desmina glared down at her and said, "I wish I was, because if it wasn't true then I would kill you on the spot for what you did to my Cyrus… But since you are who you are, I'll let you live; I wouldn't want 'him' angry with me."

Tears ran down Sarain's cheeks, as she thought of her grandfather's warning, and recalled hearing nearly nothing of her father from her mother growing up. She thought of everything; the incredible coincidence of meeting Aion so abruptly, and how he played dumb when she had questioned him about the Ancient, and realized that none of it was accidental. And then she thought of her strength, her recent headaches, and the occasional flare ups of power within her, like when she defeated Sephor; she had been channeling demonic power.

"Oh god," escaped her lips as she collapsed to the ground. Desmina continued to stare down at the helpless Sarain who repeatedly mumbled to herself, "How is it even possible? How is it even possible? ... Demons and humans can't have children."

She thought of the night her clan was attacked, and how Sephor had looked at her, staring so intently in her eyes, and she knew now why he had left her alive. It wasn't because he thought she was weak and worthless, it was because he recognized her for who she was, a demon's spawn.

Sarain began to convulse on the ground, her eyes rolled back into her head and her body jerked rapidly. She felt her skin grow cold as her insides began to heat up, and she felt a strong wave of sickness come over her body. Her head banged against the ground as she violently shook, and she lost track of time. Had a minute gone by, or an hour? Perhaps it had only been a moment, Sarain was unsure. The only thing she did know was that the moment her eyes came back into focus she saw Eddie hovering above her. His mouth was moving and his eyes were full of fear. He held her against him, trying to keep her still, and taking extra care to cradle her head. Sarain tried to speak to him but found it hard to work her jaw muscles. It took awhile before she could make out what he was saying, and when sound came back it came with a high pitched whistle.

"Sarain, are you okay? Can you hear me?" Eddie repeated nervously.

Sarain stared up at him vacantly, and forced her lips to move, "…A…A…Ai…Aion," she managed to mutter out.

"Aion? Your father? Do you want me to call him?" Eddie asked her.

"No!" She quickly stammered out to Eddie's surprise.

"What do you want me to do? What's happening? What's wrong?" Eddie shouted out, so scared that he was brought to tears. Sarain stared up at him unsure of how to respond. She wasn't sure if she even had the strength to tell him, and didn't know if she even wanted to. How could she tell him that she had demon blood in her veins? How could she tell anyone, when she didn't want to believe it herself?

"Des...Desmina?" she asked him, wondering what had become of the beast. "She's gone, she must have fled while we were out," he answered.

"Ja...James?" she worried. Eddie quickly glanced around and said, "I don't know, I checked on you first." Sarain's heart raced knowing that James had taken quite the beating, but in moments she saw his face hovering above Eddie's and he said, "I'm here." His face was bloody; his cheek was bruised, his brow was cut, and his lip was busted open. Sarain couldn't see the damage James' body had taken, but noticed that he stood hunched over with his arm clinging to his ribs; she suspected that a few of them may have been bruised or broken by his posture.

She looked back at Eddie and saw dried blood running down his forehead, he seemed worn and a bit out of breath, but otherwise in better shape than James. He must have been knocked unconscious when he hit the wall, and was probably lucky for it. He helped Sarain sit up as she began to come around. Things were starting to clear, and Sarain wondered if she had had another seizure or if she had merely gone into shock.

"Are you alright?" Eddie asked with concern, "What happened?"

Sarain searched her thoughts, she knew clearly what had taken place, but didn't know how to say it, "Desmina and I fought," she muttered, "She overpowered me."

"Why did she leave you alive?" he questioned. Sarain looked up at him and lied, "I don't know."

When they mustered the strength, they staggered home. James limply went on his own way, without so much as a goodbye, when they came to a fork in the road.

He looked as though he would need many days to heal, even with his increased healing speed, and Sarain wondered about her own.

Sarain and Eddie went back to her house, and cleaned up. Eddie washed the dried blood from his face while Sarain sat on her bed trying to shut out the thoughts of what had unfolded that night.

She changed clothes, and lay still as Eddie held her until he fell asleep. Her mind never stopped running, and once she realized that Eddie was fast and deeply asleep, she crept out of bed, and made her way to her closet. She opened the door slowly and reached quietly for the mirror. When she held it in her hands, she crept out the room, closing the bedroom door behind her. Sarain sat down on one of her living room chairs and held out the black mirror into her view. She gazed at the crack running along the glass, and prayed that the mirror still worked; she needed answers.

"Grandfather," she whispered at the object, "Grandfather, I need you." Sarain stared into the blackness of the mirror, but saw only her own reflection. She lightly shook the mirror then waited, hoping that it would make a difference, but it didn't. She stared blankly at the once enchanted object, and sighed; it was useless.

Sarain got up and placed the broken mirror on her table. She gave it one last glance and then sighed again, mumbling, "This crazy, I'm talking to a mirror, and my father might be a demon."

She began to walk back to her bedroom, and when her hand reached for the door she heard a voice call out to her; "So you finally know."

Sarain stopped in her tracks then slowly turned around. The black mirror was elevated and floating upright, above the table, with Delmar's image reflecting out. She took a deep breath and said, "It's true then? Aion is this Ancient beast?"

"He's one of many," Delmar remarked, "He's not the only of his kind, but his blood is pure." Sarain gave her grandfather a puzzled look, "I don't understand. How can his blood be pure if he's a demon? And how can he walk in daylight?"

Delmar gazed out at his granddaughter and answered, "Because, child, he wasn't made by another demon." "How can that be?" she quickly asked still confused. He sighed with frustration and explained,

"Your father is an old being, though he may look youthful, it's likely that he's much older than even me. The type of creature your father is, is the purest of demons. Yes, I know he looks human, and can walk in daylight, but that's because the change to demon was all by his own choosing."

Sarain felt a chill go down her spine, and she asked, "Why would anyone choose to become a demon?" "There are many reasons for that," Delmar replied, "Greed, lust, hate… things like these can drive a man to dark places, but when a person's soul becomes so tainted because of these things something changes inside them… And they become something else."

"How?" she simply asked. "By losing their soul… or selling it, either way, once their soul is gone that void is filled by all the sin and darkness that was in that person, and it grows… They are no longer human by this point, they are a creature of darkness, but their blood hasn't become polluted with cross-breeding or infection; it is still like human, only stronger, making them as powerful as a demon, but without any of the weaknesses," Delmar answered.

Sarain was quiet as she took it all in, she waited a moment, taking time to think, and then she asked her grandfather, "What am I?" He looked at her with a steady gaze and said, "I don't know."

Sarain shook her head with frustration, "… You knew all this time that my father was a demon, and you said nothing to me!"

"I didn't know what to do. I could find nothing to explain your existence, and besides your eyes, you appeared to be a normal child... Your mother wanted to raise you, and believed that being brought up within the clan would keep any possible demonic features of yours dormant," he relayed.

Sarain was silent, something Delmar had said caught her attention, "'She wanted to raise me', but you didn't, did you?" Her grandfather didn't respond, so Sarain continued on by asking, "And what would have happened if my demonic blood had become apparent? What would you have done to me then?"

"... Nothing ever happened, and besides, with time I grew to love you, just as any grandparent does with their child's child," Delmar responded with a stiff tone. Sarain gazed up at her grandfather, she smirked at him, and then shook her head and said, "That's a lie, you never loved me... I could always feel your hateful stare beating down on me."

"My stare was never hateful, only a watchful eye; making sure you stayed my daughter's child and not a creature, that's why I raised you to be the strong demon hunter that you are today. So that you would be able to fight off any possible urges from your demonic blood," Delmar proclaimed. Sarain glared up at the stern man and replied, "But you didn't raise me, you died. And I am the strong person I am today, because of that... I raised myself."

She began to back away from the mirror, and Delmar muttered, "...Sarain." But she didn't let him speak, she quickly said, "My father may be a demon, but I don't know what you are."

Sarain went for the door once again, this time she did not look back; she turned the knob and closed the door behind her.

Chapter 19

Sarain woke early the next morning with the sun's rays barely peeking through the trees, letting light into her bedroom. The light was dim, but more than enough to make the room entirely visible to her. Eddie remained sleeping at her side, a light bruise was on his forehead from the fight the night before. Sarain touched his skin gently; the bruise would take days to fade completely, but she knew that if it had been on her skin, the scar would barely stay; bruises only lasted heartbeats for her.

Sarain studied Eddie's peacefully sleeping face; he was always so kind and loving towards her, she could never understand why, but she couldn't bear have him look upon her knowing the truth about her origins. She feared he would no longer view her the same way, and though she so badly wanted to confide in Eddie, she couldn't.

Sarain slowly rose out of bed, careful to not stir Eddie, and dressed in her normal attire. She left her bedroom, and the first thing to catch her eye, as she found herself on the other side of the door, was the black mirror lying on the table. It no longer was elevated, it just laid there, cracked, but like any other mirror; empty of visions or reflections of the dead. Sarain left it, and simply walked past the mirror, and to the front door. Her hand gripped the cold metal of the knob, and she turned the door open.

Sarain stepped out into the day, the fresh air was cold, the sky had a dim somewhat faded brightness to it, and the ground was covered with dew. The air smelled of rain and was heavy with moisture. There was a thin fog in the atmosphere, and the streets were quiet. The morning felt peaceful as Sarain descended the stairs to her door. She wasn't exactly sure where she was going, but she knew what she was looking for: her father. She needed answers, and he was the only one who could give them to her.

She would first try the Lazy Days Inn, where he had claimed to be staying, after that she would try the tavern they had gone to, he had claimed he had an informant there. If neither of these places panned out then she would roam the streets until she found him. Sarain had to find Aion, she knew he was the key to everything, she just didn't know what she would do with him once she found him.

The day went by slowly with every place searched and every dark corner checked. The Lazy Days Inn was an immediate bust; they had never seen or heard of Aion. The tavern only remembered Aion, because they had remembered Sarain, and had only ever seen him with her.

After that, Sarain checked alleys and abandoned buildings, and though she did manage to find a couple of weak demons squatting in some of these places, she found no signs of Aion or Desmina for that matter.

The sleeping demons were easier to kill during the day; they seemed slower and weaker than usual. It didn't take more than a machete strike to take these beasts down. Sarain debated hunting more often during the day; it took more leg work, but the actual fighting was simpler.

Even with a few kills already under her belt for the day, Sarain still felt like a failure for not finding Aion. It was obvious he didn't want to be found, and Sarain wondered if Aion was already aware that she knew the truth about him. She wondered if he was somewhere with Desmina, she did know of him after all, but she wasn't sure what ties they may have had to one another, or if they just knew each other by reputation.

Sarain contemplated, and remembered that when Desmina had gotten a good look at her, she had assumed that Sarain had been there because of the Ancient. She knew that they were the ones who killed Cyrus, so if she thought they were there because of Aion, then that must have meant there was bad blood between them. Sarain wondered: her father had claimed to be a demon hunter, was it possible that he too killed his own kind, or was that just a front?

The day turned to night, and by then Sarain had grown tired and full of disappointment. She had decided to head home, and had started walking back in the direction of her house. The air had become even colder than it had been that morning, and the breeze pierced through her clothes and chilled her to the bone. She wished she had worn a jacket as she hurried her steps.

Streetlights switched on and the dark streets illuminated. The streets glistened as light reflected off the damp roads. To a child it would probably look beautiful, but to Sarain it lacked luster; she had seen so much darkness, that beauty hardly ever stood out to her. She looked up to the sky, and saw no stars; the light of the street lamps drowned them out. She continued to stare on forward, and made her way closer to home.

Sarain rounded the corner and her house came into sight. The first thing she noticed was that no lights were on in her home; Eddie must have left. The second was the form of a man sitting on her steps. She couldn't tell who it was, but she approached him with caution. Eddie could have left, locked up, came back, and was waiting for Sarain, or it could perhaps be her father; Aion had paid her a surprise visit before.

Sarain's hand was on the hilt of her machete, which was strapped into its sheath at her side. She stepped quietly towards her house, careful to not draw attention to herself. Her steps were light and soft, nearly silent, a human definitely wouldn't hear it, but when the person's head turned in her direction, Sarain knew that her visitor wasn't human. But she also knew that her visitor wasn't Aion, when the eyes that stared back at her glowed green.

Sarain gave a slight smile in his direction, and muttered, "James."

He stood up as she approached him, and as she got closer she saw the scars on his body. He stood up with a hunch; his ribs still obviously bothered him. His lip was still cut as was his brow, but his bruising was light.

"Are you still in pain?" Sarain asked with concern. "Of course, even vil sangs need time to heal... But you look good, I guess I was worried for nothing," James remarked.

Sarain gave a light shrug and said, "I didn't really get all that hurt." James glanced at her with confusion in his eyes, "But Desmina got away, and you were on the ground... What happened?"

Sarain started to shrug again, but half way through she felt her lower lip quiver, James noticed this right away. He moved quickly to Sarain's side and asked, "What's wrong?"

She shook her head and replied, "Nothing," as her eyes began to well up with disagreement. "This doesn't look like nothing," he stated looking at the expression on her face. James took Sarain by the arm and said, "Here, have a seat," then led her to the stairs. They sat down and Sarain tried to shuffle her emotions away, but she wasn't fooling James.

"Come on, you look like you need to talk," James told her, "There's nothing you can't tell me." Sarain gazed up at him, and wondered if what he said was true. This man was a vil sang, demonic blood through and through, yet still he tried to lead the life of a decent man. He of all people should have an understanding of what she was going through, and how could he really judge her for suddenly being different.

Sarain took a deep breath, and when she spoke her voice was weak, but she continued to speak, "Last night… The reason Desmina got away… was because I started to have a break down…" James gazed at her curiously, waiting for her to continue. "And I had this breakdown because of something she said," Sarain added.

"What could she have said that was so horrible?" he asked. Sarain glanced at him briefly, then adverted her eyes and replied, "She told me something about my father…" James nodded for her to go on, aware that Sarain was having trouble getting the words out. Sarain strained to talk as tears began to roll out of her eyes and suddenly she blurted out, "She told me that my father is a demon! And that I'm one too!"

A look of shock came over his face, and James quickly asked, "Could she have been lying?" She shook her head and answered, "I don't think so… I don't know how it's possible, but I'm pretty sure it's true… Besides it would explain a lot of strange things about me." "What kind of things?" he asked inquisitively.

Sarain avoided his stared, and answered, "My eye color for one, my fast healing for another: My strength, my speed, headaches that I've been getting, and most likely my visions."

James didn't respond right away, instead he thought over what she had listed and then remarked, "I did get bad headaches when I was first infected, and as I changed. They lasted for a little while but not forever… I guess since you were born with it, your body was strong enough to fight off the infection this long, but you might be starting to change."

Hearing this made Sarain flinch and the tears came out stronger. James noticed his mistake, and quickly put an arm around Sarain to try and comfort her. He said in a soft voice, "I'm sorry, I know it's not what you want to hear, but I don't want to lie to you... Look, even if you do change, which isn't even a definite, it doesn't mean you're going to turn into some horrible monster." James reached over and cupped her face with his hand and tilted her head up and said, "Look at me, I live with demonic blood every day, and I'm still able to fight demons right by your side... Nothing much has to change."

Sarain took an unsteady breath; James still held his hand to her cheek as he stared deeply into her eyes. His green eyes had a hint of luminescence to them, and though she knew that was from his demonic blood, something about them looked beautiful to her. Sarain began to lean in slightly, but James immediately moved away, letting go of her cheek. The reaction caught Sarain off guard; she had thought it was what James wanted, but now felt confused.

He looked away from her and stated, "I'd hate to take advantage of you in your moment of weakness," then he froze as though he were hit with an epiphany, and turned to her and said, "You mentioned having visions?"

"Yes?" Sarain replied puzzled. James gave her a funny look and commented, "That's not a demon thing, or at least not a common one. I've never had a vision, nor have any the other vil sangs I've known."

The comment caught Sarain by surprised, she then remarked, "Actually, my father said he was unfamiliar with visions as well. I just assumed it was a lie."

"Could you have gotten it from your mother? I mean she had to be something out of the norm anyway for you to even be born; demons and humans can't breed with each other," James replied.

"I really don't know much about my mother, besides that she was my clan's healer. She died when I was young," she answered.

"She was a healer? Well that's got to be how you happened," James said to a confused Sarain, "If her healer's blood was strong enough, she was probably able to purify your father's blood with her own or at least enough to make you."

"That's possible?" Sarain asked. James shook his head, unsure, and answered, "That's just my guess."

Sarain pondered it over; with all the crazy things she had seen, it did sound feasible. And surely she would have received just as much of her mother's blood as her father's, and with her own healer's blood fighting off the demonic blood inside of her, perhaps that was why she didn't show symptoms until now. It would also explain why she could never heal others like her mother was able to; her blood was too busy trying to heal itself.

Sarain wiped her tears and actually smiled at James, "I think you figured it out," she told him. And unlike her usual self, she reached over and hugged James;

Sarain was never much for hugging, the cheerful act was normally lost on her, but in this moment she understood why someone might do it.

As Sarain pulled away from a surprised James, her eyes immediately went to the man standing at the bottom of the steps, a very displeased Eddie.

Chapter 20

Eddie stared down at them with an expression Sarain had never seen on his face before. He looked completely furious. He was quiet for a moment, and when he finally spoke, he said, "You left so suddenly this morning, that I thought I should come back after work and check on you... I didn't think you would have company."

Sarain glanced at James and then back at Eddie and muttered, "It's not what you think." He glared down at her and stated, "I think a lot of things; how do you know what I'm thinking?"

James quickly stood up; he looked to Sarain as though trying to figure out how to react. For a moment Sarain thought James was going to get defensive, a look like he thought he had to protect her came over his face, but then James thought better of it. Instead he glanced down and said aloud, "I should probably get going." He then stepped around Eddie who ignored him, and abruptly went on his way.

Sarain stood up and glared at Eddie, "You didn't have to do that Edward." "He left on his own," Eddie remarked. Sarain ignored his comment and said, "James is my friend, and you don't have to jump down my throat every time I see him."

"Been seeing him a lot?" he asked crudely. Sarain glared at Eddie and stated, "Only when you've been around... lately." She then turned around to leave, but when she reached for her door, she stopped. Eddie saw this and quickly asked, "What is it?"

Sarain stared at the slight gap in her door, and asked, "Did you lock up?" "Of course," he answered as if called stupid. Sarain's heart began to race as she said, "Someone has been in my house."

She quickly pushed the door open and they both rushed inside. They first stepped into the living room/kitchen, but nothing looked out of place. The mirror still laid on the table and not a chair was out of place. Sarain immediately rushed to her bedroom and switched on her light.

Her closet door was left open, and her little black safe laid open and empty on the ground. Items and photos were scattered about the room, Eddie gave a glance around while Sarain frantically began cleaning up. Oddly, other than the mess nothing else appeared to be tampered with.

"Could James have done this?" he quickly asked. "Don't be stupid, he couldn't get past the barrier," Sarain replied, annoyed by his obviously jealous conclusion.

Eddie took another quick look around, then surprisingly told Sarain, "It doesn't look like there's any forced entry." "I don't think my barrier has been broken either," she replied also surprised, then added, "But I think a picture of my mother is missing."

Eddie looked down and saw a photo upside down at his feet. "Maybe this is it," he said as he bent down to pick it up.

Sarain quickly looked down at her stack of photos then suddenly called out, "Wait!" But it was too late; Eddie had already retrieved the photograph and was now studying its image.

A strange look came over his face and his skin went pale. "W...what is this?" he stammered out the words in shock. Sarain didn't answer; she didn't know what to say or how to explain. Until finally Eddie asked again, this time more specific and with rage, "Why does this guy with you in this photo look like me?"

He held out the picture of her and Orran as kids. Sarain looked at him with fear in her eyes and simply answered, "I'm sorry."

"You're sorry? For what, using me to replace some old boyfriend?" Eddie shouted at her. "It's not like that!" she cried out. "Oh, because nothing is ever how it seems with you! Right?" he yelled at her.

Eddie glared at Sarain and looked as though his eyes had finally opened, "Is this why you're always holding back from me, because I'm not this guy?" He threw the photo at her, and turned away, saying, "I'm done."

Sarain began to panic, and quickly grabbed Eddie's arm, but he yanked his arm away and shouted, "Don't even try. If it's not you pushing me away, then it's you flirting with James right in front of me; calling out his name, meeting with him in secret."

"We are just friends!" Sarain pleaded. "Bull!" Eddie suddenly said, "Friends don't look at each other that way!" Sarain then took a step back from him as he said with tears in his eyes, "Why can't you look at me that way?"

She stared at Eddie, but couldn't give him an answer. He turned away from her and stormed off. It wasn't long before Sarain heard the front door slam shut. She stood there stunned for a moment, then wiped her eyes and continued picking up the contents of her safe.

She picked up the picture of her and Orran, and stared down at it. They were just teenagers in it, but a resemblance could be seen between him and Eddie. Eddie's eyes were darker, his hair was lighter and she thought Orran might have been taller, but he looked a bit like what Sarain imaged Orran might have looked like if he had grown older. She hadn't wanted to admit it to herself before, but she did believe that her initial attraction to Eddie was because he resembled Orran. But besides them both having the urge to protect her, their personalities were completely different. Orran had always been a quiet and collected person, while Eddie was often emotional and acted rashly.

Sarain herself wondered if Eddie might be right, maybe she had used him in hopes of replacing Orran. She tried to ponder over how she truly felt about Eddie, but her mind felt so clouded that she couldn't focus.

Besides, she couldn't worry about that now. She had to worry about who had broken into her home, and with only the picture of her and her mother missing, she knew exactly who it was: Aion.

Evidently he was able to cross her barriers, since he had been in her home before. He had even recognized her barrier by scent, and though he was a demon, it did nothing to him. Like her grandfather had said, he didn't share the same weaknesses as other demons. And the fact that he had broken into her place to steal the photo, showed that he knew Sarain no longer trusted him. But it also showed that he possibly had been telling her the truth, about still loving her mother.

Sarain wondered how much of her father was still a man, and how much was a beast.

The night was still young, and Sarain needed to clear her mind. She grabbed a jacket and went outside. The air had grown colder, though so had Sarain's demeanor, so much so that she barely noticed the extra chill in the air.

She walked aimlessly. It was nowhere near dawn, but most stores had already closed. Only bars and nightclubs would be open, but Sarain wasn't sure how she felt about crowds at the moment; even at her best, she wasn't much of a people person. Besides, she could feel the anger brewing inside her, like a pit of fire in her stomach. Her head slightly ached as she walked down the empty streets.

Then she suddenly stopped in front of a closed store. She gazed up at something she had been trying to avoid, but it wasn't anything to do with the store. Before her was a large pane of glass, the store's display window. Clothed mannequins stood behind the glass, but it wasn't them that Sarain was staring at. The store was dark making the glass dark too, and more reflective. In that reflection played out a familiar scene; two people fighting a hoard of demons that were all emerging from burning wreckage. One was a blond haired man with pale skin, and the other was a dark haired woman; Winston and Sarain.

Sarain watched as the two of them fought the demons, and saw the small creature sneaking up behind her that she hadn't seen the first time around. It stabbed her in the back, but she kept fighting. Then she staggered, and as she watched herself fall, she also saw Winston catch her, but something was left out. Sarain had remembered seeing a bright light after having been stabbed, and hearing her mother's voice, but as the scene played out in the glass, none of that was shown. She knew what she had seen, but the vision did not capture it, and instead, all she could see was the worried and loving way Winston stared down at her.

She began to ball her fists and felt as though she were being punished, constantly reminded of how she abandoned Winston. She had rejected him, because of his demonic blood, and now she learned that her blood too was tainted; an ironic twist of fate. But she also wondered if she was being shown this particular scene not only to remind her of what she had done to one man who had loved her, but also of what she was doing to another.

Sarain knew she was pushing Eddie away, whether she meant to or not.

Sarain was tired of being faced with her past, it was infuriating. Whether or not it could help her with her issues with Eddie, Sarain no longer wanted to see her past deeds. Her eyes let the scene go out of focus, it blurred, and her eyes began to burn. Then they focused on something else; her own reflection. Not a memory or a vision, but her own present image, and she saw something she didn't like.

Her violet eyes were glowing.

Chapter 21

Sarain scowled and swiftly pulled out her machete. She swung at the glass and it shattered into pieces. The tiny shards sparkled as they fell to the ground with each one catching the light from the streetlamps. An alarm soon sounded, and it echoed out a shrill whistle. Sarain stood there staring at the debris, and thinking of how the large glass had so easily crumbled. It was all that kept anyone from entering the store, and it had been so effortless to break. It seemed futile to Sarain; it was too fragile to be of any use.

Sarain wondered if she too was breaking easily. She had fought many monsters, and as soon as the thought that she might be one of them entered her mind, she suddenly felt helpless and hopeless. Her life was losing meaning, and nothing made sense.

More than a minute went by before Sarain felt a pair of hands on her shoulders, jogging her out of her trance. The hands spun her around before she could react, and she found herself face to face with a worried friend. He must have stayed close by to Sarain, concerned for her.

"Come on, we have to get out of here," James quickly said. He then took Sarain by the hand and rushed her away from the scene of the crime. Sirens rang out, and she glimpsed the flashing of red and blue lights. The first thing that came to her mind was if Eddie was in the car.

James pulled Sarain into an alley then quickly peeked out. He turned to her, and said, "They're not following; I don't think they saw us." He then stared at the cowering Sarain and asked her, "Why did you do that?"

She looked up at him and could feel her eyes still burning. After that James could see why she was upset, and simply responded, "Oh." He took a step towards Sarain, and placed a hand on her back then said, "It caught me off guard the first time too." James then grazed his hand down Sarain's arm and took her by the hand once more. He lightly tugged on her arm and muttered, "We should get out of here. They might search the area."

Sarain gazed up at him and said, "I know a place we can go."

Sarain led the way without a word. She continued to hold on to James' hand, and didn't let go of it until they reached their destination. She normally wasn't a hand holder, but she liked being able to feel that he was still there beside her.

She stopped in front of an abandoned warehouse downtown. The building was marked with a simple red X spray painted on the brick. James turned to her and asked, "You go here?" Sarain looked back at him and replied, "I have a business arrangement with the owners."

"They're demonic vil sangs, this is a vil sang club," James pointed out the obvious. Sarain smiled at him a bit amused, and remarked, "I know... I thought you said that not all demons had to be monsters." "Yeah, but they also sell exotic meats," James replied. "I know, which includes other demons, but my arrangement with them keeps humans off the list. Besides, most of their clients live by guidelines, like yourself," Sarain relayed.

James stared at Sarain blankly until she finally asked, "What?" He just smiled at her and said, "You continue to surprise me." Sarain then took his hand and pulled James towards the X. They approached the door and it immediately swung open. Behind it stood a large bouncer whom Sarain knew was a vil sang. He immediately recognized her and let both her and James pass once he looked at James, and quickly realized that he was a vil sang.

Colorful lights flashed on and off throughout the large and crowded room. Pale bodies danced like shadows on a wall next to a roaring fire. Sarain still held James' hand as she pulled him through the crowd, and though a building as crowded as this one would normally be hot, the air felt cold.

The room was full of creatures, and Sarain was beginning to feel like one of them. She stopped in the middle of the room, surrounded by half demons, and pulled James closer to her. He stood there stiff, still unsure of why Sarain would want to go to such a place.

As if reading his mind, she leaned in to his ear and whispered, "Dance." While Sarain remained near, James' cool cheek brushed up against hers, and he replied, "Are you sure this is where you want to be?" She pulled her head back, gazed into his eyes and answered, "I'll be fine, I have you here to protect me."

Sarain started to dance first, keeping with the beat of the pulsating music. James waited a moment before following her example. It was possible that his injuries were also deterring him, but soon he moved in rhythm across from her, dancing like a wild soul with nothing to lose.

Their eyes met, and Sarain noticed that his green eyes had begun to glow, and she suspected that hers were glowing as well. She felt like an animal as she danced, swaying back and forth. Her heart raced and her eyes locked with James' again, this time they held their gaze. They both instinctively moved closer to one another until their bodies nearly touched. Then things seemed to slow down, James began to reach out and Sarain felt him take her hand. His skin was cool against hers; she still felt warm regardless of how much she felt she was changing. He pulled her closer until their bodies were touching and held her in a slow dance.

The others still danced separately and rapidly, but they didn't care, James held Sarain like they were the only two people in the room. She rested her head on his shoulder, and began to get lost in the music. Then, as if sensing his eyes, Sarain gazed up to find James staring down at her and without a word he leaned down and pressed his cold lips against Sarain's warm mouth. He kissed her softly, and she didn't pull away; she let the kiss happen and even felt herself kissing him back. Their lips now moved to the music, and their arms began to wrap around one another, holding each other tight.

Sarain's heart began to pound with adrenaline and her body grew hot. James kissed her passionately and moved his cold hands up the back of her shirt, his palms against her hot skin. Sarain felt the urge to want to take James to a more secluded spot, but fought those urges surging through her body. Instead she used her hands to push herself away from James, making some room between them. Sarain gazed up at him to see his eyes burning down at hers. She could see the hunger on his face as he began to lower his head back down to kiss her once more, and then the thought of Eddie waiting up to make up with her flashed into her mind. It was like her mind had suddenly cleared, and Eddie was all she saw inside.

Sarain pushed James away, and he quickly tried to grab for her again, but she had turned and began to shove her way through the crowd. She raced through the room with James trying to follow, not wanting to lose her in the crowd, but he couldn't keep up. Sarain knew she was upsetting him, and that he had to be confused by her actions, but it was Eddie she was more worried about. She was betraying a good man who had done nothing more than try to help and protect her from the moment they met. She needed to get back to Eddie, and make things right.

Her feelings for James would have to be dissolved, but a part of her felt that what she was feeling for him was nothing more than lust. Her lusting to take solace in a familiar way she had done once before with another creature of the night. Though she knew no matter how much she may have secretly wanted to relive a past occurrence, this was not the same man, nor was she really that same woman. James reminded her of Winston like Eddie had reminded her of Orran, but unlike James, Eddie had managed to stand out to Sarain as his own person. She saw him differently, and he no longer reminded her of her old friend.

Sarain ran out of the X and into the cold night air. She treaded with one foot in front of the other, and headed in the direction of her house. She knew she was grasping at straws, but a part of her hoped to find Eddie waiting for her at her home. She just wondered if she would be too late. Eddie was always coming back, he was always forgiving her, and Sarain hoped that he would do so one more time.

Her feet splashed through puddles, and her breathing turned heavy as she raced to get home. Streetlights blurred by, and car horns blared as she cut through traffic. She rounded the corner to her house with both fear and hope in her heart. She took a deep breath as she turned the corner.

Her house stood dark and vacant, with no sign of a visitor waiting for her. Sarain let her breath go as her eyes began to well up. It was her own fault; she had used up all her chances, and finally chased Eddie away.

She slowly made her way to her door, both slowed by disappointment and tired from the exertion of running home. She took the steps carefully and opened up her door with no sign of Eddie ever having come back. At least she knew that she hadn't missed him, but the idea that he hadn't even tried to make up with her only made her feel worse. She closed the door behind her, and headed straight for her bedroom. She thought about calling Eddie, but wondered if it would be too soon, and if he would even answer. She looked to her clock and saw that the hour was late, and decided not to pick up the phone.

Sarain collapsed on her bed, and curled up against her pillows. She could still smell his scent on her sheets. Before she knew it, her pillows were soaked with tears. She lifted her head; she hadn't realized that she was crying. She must have missed Eddie more than she thought she would. She laid her head back down on her dampened pillow and closed her eyes. She wanted to sleep the rest of the night away, and wake up to yesterday, and then maybe she could get the day right.

Sarain waited for sleep and hoped for peaceful dreams.

Her long dark hair fluttered in the breeze; strands flowed silkily through the air, and curled at the ends; but it wasn't her hair that caught the attention of the man behind the counter, it was the sparkling of her brown eyes. The man was so captivated by her eyes that he didn't even notice the small child whose hand she was holding or the older man by her side, glaring at him profusely.

The older man pulled the woman along gruffly and out of sight of the store clerk. Her little girl nearly tripped, still trying to cling to her mother's hand. She lost grip of her mother and started to cry. The older man quickly took hold of the child, and muttered something to her in a harsh tone. Though all that the clerk could make out was the man telling the girl to keep her eyes down, and he thought that it was a strange request to make to a child.

The younger man's attention quickly went back to the woman who was also trying to avert her eyes; she wasn't used to being stared at by strangers; in fact, she wasn't used to strangers at all. Her father rarely let her leave their clan's barriers, and this was the first time her daughter had ever crossed the barrier for something other than a clan move.

The clerk smiled at the pretty woman, and she blushed as she tried to hide behind a display. The tall older man looked up at the clerk and saw him staring at his daughter. He glared at the younger man with his dark stern eyes, and soon the clerk took notice of it, and his face went pale.

The older man pushed the child into his daughter's direction and immediately said loudly, "Keep an eye on your daughter!" The woman cradled her child in her arms, and glared up at her father; she knew he was trying to embarrass her, but she could never be embarrassed of her beautiful daughter. She wiped her child's tears away, and gave her a smile. The little girl smiled sweetly up at her mother, and for a moment the clerk could have sworn he saw a glint of purple in the girl's eyes, but then assured himself that it must have been a trick of light.

The store door rang with a bell as it suddenly swung opened. The little girl's head immediately turned towards the sound of the noise, and then she felt her mother's firm grip quickly clamp down on her.

The new arrival was not a customer; it was a man wearing a black ski mask pulled down over his face. He held a gun in his hand and raised it so all could see before pointing it at the clerk and saying, "If everybody stays calm, and gives me their money, then no one will get hurt." The little girl looked to her mother for instruction, but only saw her mother exchanging worried glances with her grandfather.

The woman glanced down at her daughter then back to her father. He stood there frozen, unsure of how to proceed in the situation. The masked robber stood diagonal from the older man, with him slightly behind the thief. The robber had walked right past him when entering the store and the woman wasn't sure if the thief had even seen her father; the ski mask appeared to have left him in his blind spot.

She motioned to her father with her eyes, and hoped that he would do something to stop the robber, but instead he just stood there staring back at his daughter, and after a moment he simply averted his eyes altogether.

The thief stepped closer towards the clerk at the register, pointing his gun at him all the while. The woman watched as the clerk nervously emptied the register. His hands shook with each handful of money he shoveled into a brown paper bag, and for a second his eye caught the woman's and she could see the fear in him. The clerk quickly glanced away from the woman, hoping not to draw attention to her, but the split second they shared was long enough to catch the robber's eye. He turned around and saw both the woman and her father. He immediately pointed the gun at the older man and instructed, "Move back, you're too close." He then turned his attention to the woman, and asked, "You're a pretty little thing, what's your name?"

"Leave her alone," the clerk abruptly said to even his own surprise. The thief tensed up in anger and quickly stated, "Did I say you could talk?" He suddenly spun around to face the clerk once again, but in his frustration accidentally pressed down on the trigger of the gun. It went off with a deafening blast, and the thief stood there in shock for a moment before finally grabbing the half full bag of money, and running out the door. The door rang with a bell as it swung shut and rattled from the force that had thrust it. The child screamed and cried out in fear of the loud and unfamiliar noise. Her mother stared in fright as she saw the clerk bloody and slumped over the register, but it only took her a second to realize that he was still breathing.

Her hands unclamped from her crying daughter's shoulders, and she quickly rushed to the store clerk's aid. Her father knew what she was about to do, and he promptly shouted out, "No Ariana!" Her hands had already started heating up, and as she reached to place them onto the clerk, she felt a pair of strong hands grab her by the waist and pull her away.

"No," Ariana shouted as her father dragged her towards the door, "I can save him!" "And everyone would find out about us!" Delmar declared. He wrapped his arm around his daughter's waist to hold her back and then picked up Sarain with his free arm. Her father was a strong man that Ariana knew she couldn't fight. She knew she could have saved the clerk, but as she strained to see him slumped over the counter, she saw his eyes staring back at her as they began to turn glassy. Delmar pulled her out the door just as she saw the man take his last breath. She would never forgive her father for letting the man die; she would never forgive herself for being too weak to fight him.

Sarain shot up in bed, wondering if her dream had been real. She couldn't remember that far back, and didn't feel as though it was her memory. She felt as though she had just seen through her mother's eyes.

Sarain exhaled and tried to relax, but after a moment she only tensed up more once she realized she wasn't alone. She stared across the room at the figure standing by the foot of her bed, and muttered, "Aion."

Chapter 22

"I really wish you'd call me, 'Father'," Aion simply stated. Sarain glared up at him and remarked, "I would never call a thing, 'Father'. You lied to me."

"I only stretched the truth a little; I am a hunter of sorts, and I am your father after all," he continued to press. "We may share the same blood, but you aren't my father; you didn't raise me," Sarain insisted.

"And the man who did, was he really any more a father than me?" he asked with a strange resentful tone in his voice. "He may not have been a nice man, but he wasn't a cold blooded killer like yourself," she stated, still reflecting on her dream, but understanding Delmar's urge to protect his family.

"I wouldn't be so quick to defend a man you clearly didn't truly know," Aion remarked harshly. "Why should I listen to you? You murdered my clan, didn't you?" Sarain began to shout. It made the most sense to her; the night her clan was attacked, the demons somehow got past her clans holy and ritualistic barriers that should have kept them out. Aion had now for the third time crossed her house's barrier without a fuss.

"I know it was you, you're the only one I've ever known to be able to cross a holy barrier. How did you do it?" Sarain pleaded in disturbance. Aion sighed, seemingly out of frustration, and explained nonchalantly, "It's really quite a simple trick once you've managed to build up as much power as I have. And once something evil has tainted a barrier by crossing over it, it can no longer hold any other out."

"So you admit you are evil, and that you murdered my clan?" she quickly announced with a questioning tone. "I admit that I was once young and naïve, and so hungry for power that, yes, I sold my soul, but I had no idea what that meant at the time," Aion said with a sympathetic voice.

"Don't try to make me feel sorry for you! Even if that was true, you still had to know what you were doing when you ordered the murder of my clan," Sarain shouted at him.

"You make it sound like I'm some monster bent on murdering the good. Yes, I may have used my influence on weaker demons, to make myself an army, and yes, I ordered them to abolish your clan, but I was not murdering innocent victims," Aion remarked as though talking down to a child.

"What else would you call it, when demons kill helpless women and children?" she cried out. "It's called getting rid of future soldiers loyal to an evil man," he replied staring down at his daughter.

"You call my grandfather 'an evil man', compared to you?" Sarain said with so much surprise that she nearly laughed.

"Well, in all of my years as a demon, I may have killed many people, but I've never murdered my own child," Aion replied to Sarain's disbelief. She didn't believe what she was hearing, and quickly stated, "My mother died of a long terminal illness, even if he had anything to do with her finally passing, it would have only been an act of compassion and sympathy to her pain."

"Delmar constantly ruled over your mother's life, he made her this picture of a perfect saintly creature who could never step out of line," he started to say, but Sarain interrupted by asking, "And what's wrong with wanting the best for your child?"

"But that's not what he wanted, he kept his daughter in line, because she was the reason he became chief of your clan. If he hadn't been blessed with a daughter with the ability to heal, the clan would have never seen him as anything other than another soldier," Aion added. Sarain sighed with frustration, and pleaded, "Why does any of this matter? I know the kind of tyrant he could be, and maybe he wasn't the best father, but he couldn't help his daughter getting sick."

"Don't you realize it? Ariana was a powerful healer; she was able to give birth to a child that went against the natural order of life. Demons, whether by blood or damnation can't conceive with humans, our blood works as a virus in them, but her blood was strong enough to fight that virus and make my seed into a child.

Blood that strong can't get sick by natural means," Sarain remained quiet as Aion continued, but was starting to see where her father was going with his remarks. "The only way she could get sick, would be by massive poisoning, constantly, and over a long period of time. Otherwise her body would be able to fight it off and cure itself. And the only person able to get close enough to her to pull off such a thing would have been her father," he finished with Sarain's heart beginning to race.

"But... why would he kill his own daughter?" she mumbled almost to herself. "If he couldn't keep her in line, and if she had become disillusioned to his ways, then she would have become a threat to his title as clan chief. The people would have looked to her for leadership, but with her out of the way, they would remain unaware and following his word alone," Aion explained, "Much like any ruler at war."

"No... They may have fought, and his punishments might have been too harsh, but he loved my mother, he never would have killed her," Sarain spoke weakly, more trying to assure herself than Aion.

"You've been seeing him in that black mirror you have here, haven't you? Don't you ever wonder why you haven't seen Ariana or anyone else you may have loved in that mirror?" Aion remarked to her as though knowing her thoughts. She looked up at her father and asked, "How do you know that?"

Aion gave a slight smile and replied, "It's an easy guess, knowing that a black mirror can only show you souls in purgatory, and a truly good or innocent person doesn't wind up there in limbo. Only those trapped after a life of misdeeds done under the belief of righteousness ever go there. People who murder for their religion or under some assumption that it's right, people who use their holy position over others to fulfill twisted desires; these are the ones who end up in purgatory, because they don't understand what they did was wrong, and can usually find some way to rationalize it."

"Well, by these standards, you should go to purgatory yourself," Sarain relayed to her father. "No, I would go to hell, but lucky for me that's only if I die, it's not really a when. But I had only ever been a greedy, power hungry man before I met Delmar. No, it wasn't until him that I ever truly hated. When he took your mother away from me I swore vengeance on him, but when I learned that he murdered her, that's when I stopped caring about who got hurt along the way. I may have already lost my soul before then, but it wasn't until him that I became a monster," Aion said, no longer looking at his daughter, but recalling a different time.

"Didn't you care about what would happen to me?" Sarain asked like a helpless child. "I didn't even know that you existed until the night of the attack, when a loyal servant relayed the tale of an incredibly strong child with violet eyes, ripping out the heart of one of my soldiers. And I've been searching for you ever since," Aion answered her, and Sarain recalled the intense stare she had received from Sephor that night, the one that had burned its way into her memory when she met him again, years ago.

"But how did you even find out about my mother's death?" she asked confused. "We demons can feel such an unholy act as murdering one of your own. Killing your own child is the kind of thing one would do to become a demon, and he only did it for mortal power," Aion stated.

Sarain's eyes began to well up at the thought of her dysfunctional family. She prayed that what Aion was saying was lies, but in her heart she felt that it was true. "Why are you even here? Why hurt me by telling me this?!" she shouted at her father.

"You needed to know the truth," Aion replied and then he told her, "And because I want you to come with me." "Why?" she asked weakly. "You are my only child," he said lovingly, "And you don't belong with these people… Humans are just as tainted and wicked as demons, but they are weak, and they kill for lesser reasons like jealously and greed."

"But you sold your soul because of greed," she pointed out. "Yes, when I was human," Aion stated, "But what I've learned and become since then is something so much greater." "But demons kill for sport," Sarain insisted. "Yes some do, but like any species, there is always a weaker link," Aion continued to persist.

Sarain looked to her father, full of complexity, and said, "No, I want a normal life, I want a family." He stared down at her displeased and said, "You aren't one of them, you could never lead a normal life… And as for a family…" Aion started to say, but stopped. Sarain stared at him with perplexity and questioned, "What were you going to say?"

Her father's expression looked solemn. He contemplated for a moment before finally telling her, "Your body is not like your mother's; you may have healer's blood in you, but the demon blood in you is not like a regular virus; it's engrained in your DNA." "I know that I'm changing, I've seen it, but what does that really mean?" she asked him.

"You're becoming something else; not human, but not quite demon. Whatever it is, it's putting a toll on your healer blood. It's barely maintaining you as is, the idea of you having a child doesn't seem possible," her father finally relayed; he knew more about her than she possibly could.

Sarain's skin went cold, and she asked, "Am I becoming a vil sang?" Aion took a moment before answering, "Maybe, I'm not sure, but that's why I want you to come with me. Whatever you're turning into, I can help you deal with it."

Sarain sat there in silence and Aion told her, "I will give you time to think it over, but I won't wait forever. I plan to leave town soon, and you need to decide before then whether or not you'll be coming with me." With that her father left her in peace, and Sarain sat there in disbelief.

Nothing was what she thought it was; yes her father murdered her clan, but out of grief, because Delmar had murdered his own daughter. Sarain wasn't sure if she could still hate her father after seeing how truly alike they were; he had murdered her clan, because of what one had done to someone he had loved, and she murdered demons, because what they had done to those she loved. She had met many nasty humans in her line of work as she had also met kind and helpful vil sangs like James and Winston. The line between good and evil had blurred over the years, and what was once black and white had turned gray.

Sarain didn't know what choice she planned to make, but knew she had little time to do so.

Chapter 23

Sarain laid in bed for most of the day, contemplating her life. She had lost Eddie, she had no family, and she was turning into something she didn't understand; all she had was her father, and he wanted to take care of her, but she wasn't sure if she could trust him. He didn't live the life of a good man, but Sarain herself wasn't a saint. Aion killed her innocent clan members, but she may have killed many innocent vil sangs; she never used to stop to ask. Perhaps she could learn from her father, she could go with him and if things didn't feel right she could go back to being on her own.

This wasn't a decision she wanted to take lightly. Sarain finally got up and dressed herself. She ate and cleaned up, and by the time she was ready to step outside, it had already become dark.

She opened her door and the cool night air came rushing in, and as she took her first step outside, she immediately stopped and looked down at the figure sitting on her steps. It was James sitting there patiently, hoping to see Sarain. He stood up abruptly, and looked up at her with concern.

"I was worried that something was wrong, you left so suddenly last night. I thought, I mean, did I do something wrong?" James asked her with a nervous tone. Sarain closed the door behind her, and walked down her steps. She stopped and turned to James and answered, "It wasn't you, I just have a lot going on right now."

James sighed in relief, he then extended his hand out to Sarain, and tried to hold her hand, but she quickly moved it away. His expression changed, the smile that was forming disappeared, and was replaced by a look of sadness. Sarain averted her eyes and explained, "I'm sorry, I just can't right now. It's too soon."

James looked away as well and muttered, "I understand," but his tone said differently. She quickly glanced at him and stated, "Maybe you should go." James was silent for a moment, and then he suddenly said, "Well, that's not the only reason I'm here."

Sarain stared up at him and asked, "What is it?" He gazed back at her, a serious look on his face, and said, "I found Desmina." "You did? Where is she?" Sarain asked with astonishment. "She's in another abandoned building across town, staying in its basement. She obviously doesn't know how to change her routine without Cyrus," James responded.

Sarain looked at James, suddenly rejuvenated with purpose, and stated, "We should go now." He stopped her for a second and questioned, "Don't you want to wait for… back up or something." Sarain noticed the pause and knew he meant to say Eddie's name. She looked up at him and replied without further explanation, "It's just you and me now." "Oh," he simply remarked.

She then glanced at him again and asked, "Are you ready?" James stared back at her and answered, "Anything for you."

James led the way with Sarain clutching her favorite machete. They weren't much of a match for Desmina the first time, and now they were down a man, but this time there would be no shocking Sarain, no catching her off guard. She knew what and who she was, and she was going to use it to her advantage. Desmina was a fierce demon, and the only way Sarain could hope to destroy her would be to draw from her own demon blood.

As Sarain followed James, there was a moment when everything felt clear; she was still on her mission, nothing had changed. She was fighting with another hunter by her side, and preparing to extinguish the evil, just as she had always been taught. But that moment of clarity fogged, and Sarain remembered that the hunter by her side was part demon as well as she, and that everything she had been taught was done by a man who ruled over her with fear and lies.

The moon shone down on them as Sarain and James crept near the old condemned building with Desmina lurking somewhere inside. It had once been an orphanage, but after a scandal, had closed down many years ago. Sarain found it disturbing that a monster would choose to stay in a place that once housed so many children.

James stopped at the storm doors leading down into the basement, and turned to Sarain. She knew that he meant to continue down those stairs, but for a moment,

James stood gazing at her, as if it may be his last. He didn't say a word, worried that anything said at this point could be heard by the beast down below. He simply extended out his hand and stroked Sarain softly across her cheek. She trembled slightly from the chill of his skin, and gazed into his kind green eyes, wondering why he cared for her so. James then gave her a weak smile and turned back around to proceed down the stairs.

They stepped softly and silently, careful not to make the old steps creak. The basement stood in blackness, but Sarain felt her eyes adjusting to the dark more quickly than they should have been, if she was entirely human. The basement was large, and ran the full length of the house. It had been converted into an underground faux playground with trees and flowers painted on the walls. Fake clouds and a bright yellow sun also decorated the cellar, though the paint had faded and chipped over the many years. A rusty swing set lay broken in pieces on the ground, and Sarain noticed that the concrete had been spray painted green to look like grass. She wondered if the children who had once lived here had ever been allowed to play outside; the overdone playroom told her a tale of captivity.

James stepped over the debris as he searched around the dark corridor for their adversary. The large room appeared empty until Sarain spotted a door in the back, painted to look like a skyscraper and to blend into the scenery. She waved her arm to grab James' attention and motioned to the door. He nodded and headed with her towards it. As they approached the door, Sarain extended her hand out slowly to the knob, and turned it as quietly as she could. It clicked louder than expected and she immediately held her breath in reflex. Sarain quickly swung the door open, when she realized that she had to move fast. James raised his blade, as did Sarain, but then she stopped hers in midair, and looked down at the floor in puzzlement. Sitting there calmly was Desmina; the large gray beast sat waiting patiently with no intention to move and just looked up at them with her lime green eyes.

Sarain lowered her blade slightly, but not completely, wondering what game Desmina could be playing. The creature stared up at her and it muttered, "I was once a delicate girl like yourself... a long time ago." Sarain stared blankly back at the demon, but said nothing in reply, so Desmina continued by saying, "Time has taken the joy out of my life, and now with Cyrus gone, I don't see much point in carrying on like this."

Desmina glanced up at Sarain and said to her, "You might as well use that thing in your hand, I won't stop you." But Sarain didn't budge, instead she lowered her blade, and spoke to Desmina with a look of loathing on her face, "You act as though you're a victim, just because you lost your lover, and that all those people you've murdered over the years didn't even matter... Face it, everything that has happened you had coming because of your own faults."

Desmina stared up at Sarain with a look of discontent, and quickly stated, "Cyrus was my brother, not my lover! But then you obviously have no idea what the true meaning of family is; you don't even know your own!" The remark cut into Sarain like a deep wound. This beast had felt so much love for her family that she longed to die without them. Sarain didn't feel that, and she never could. She could barely remember her mother, and couldn't stand to recall her grandfather, she had no siblings, and her father was a stranger at best. With her changing body, she would never bear a child, and had no hopes of creating a family of her own to hold on to. This beast would know a love that Sarain could never have.

The creature looked pleased to see that her words hurt Sarain, but still Sarain carried on by saying, "It doesn't matter what he was to you, you have to pay for the people you killed." Desmina continued to stare up at her and said, "You think it's so simple, but wait until the hunger sets in for you... That urge to feed growing stronger and stronger, seeing how these people waste their lives, once you've lived through that and still managed not to kill then you can talk to me."

"I am not like you," Sarain muttered. Desmina grunted out a hoarse chuckle, and replied, "We are more alike than you think. Hell, we're practically family... The Ancient made me as well; though he may not be my original father, he did make me what I am today." Sarain's expression turned to one of disgust as she asked, "Why would my father ever make you?" "I guess he wanted a child... But I must have been a disappointment, since he sent you to kill me. Looks like he's finally got the child he always wanted," the beast relayed.

"Aion didn't send me, your twisted sense of love and punishment did," Sarain declared with a tone full of vigor and frustration. Desmina gazed on, amused, and asked, "And what exactly would that be?" This time Sarain was the one nearly laughing as she stated, "You've done so much evil that killing James' kids doesn't even stand out to you? Ruining his life once by turning him just wasn't enough for you!"

Desmina's expression quickly changed as she turned serious and said, "Who's James?" Sarain's mouth opened to speak, but nothing came out. She meant to say how childish it was to deny knowing a man whose life you'd ruined, when she suddenly realized that James had been the one who told her that Cyrus and Desmina were lovers. He had even claimed that Desmina had turned him as a way to make Cyrus jealous. Sarain then realized that neither Desmina nor Cyrus ever showed or said anything in recognition of James when he fought them, and surely, if he had spent time with them, he would have known if they were siblings.

Sarain stared down into Desmina's bright lime green eyes and she remembered Cyrus staring down at her in that alley with those same exact eyes. Sarain turned her attention away from Desmina, and she quickly looked over her shoulder to where she had last saw James standing. To her amazement, no one was there; Sarain stood alone with Desmina in the dark dank cellar.

James had lied to her; Sarain didn't know what was true at all.

A few minutes went by before anything was said. Sarain stared down at Desmina blankly, "Why would Aion want you dead, if he made you?" she asked the silent beast. Desmina glanced up at her and replied, "Cyrus and I were both once his children. We would do his biddings, carry out his every order, and not question him for it. Then one night he had us be part of an army, and ordered us all to murder an entire village of people. The people had wronged him in some way. In truth, I didn't really care why. I was used to murdering people by then, but he ordered Cyrus and I, specifically, to take care of the children. And when I asked him why, they were just children after all, he became enraged. He wanted everyone dead, including children and babies. I couldn't do it, but Cyrus remained loyal to him. He carried out the master's order, and gave me credit for it."

Sarain stared down at the demon with pent up anger, but conserved herself enough to ask, "Did this happen about ten years ago?" Desmina suddenly glanced up at her with recognition in her eyes and asked, "Your people?" Sarain didn't respond and simply waited for Desmina to answer, and when she did, she adverted her eyes and responded with a muttered, "Yes."

Sarain took a deep breath and swallowed down the urge to take vengeance for her clan out on the lowly beast before her, instead she questioned her by asking, "Why would Aion take so long to punish you?" Desmina didn't look up as she answered, "For a while he didn't know. But after that night I started having trouble with killing altogether. I started questioning the Ancient's motives and then eventually broke away from him... Cyrus went with me, and we began to travel from town to town... I could only bring myself to feed on criminals at that point. It was all I could do to keep my sanity... Then one day word got out about how we were living, other creatures began to despise us. I guess the Ancient found out what we were doing, I suppose he didn't want his creations tarnishing his name."

"So you believe he was the one who sent James?" Sarain remarked. Desmina gave a slight nod, "He's always sending others to do his dirty work, but he must have had him enlist your aide as well, a single regular vil sang could never be strong enough to take on both my brother and I." Sarain recollected as she said aloud, "He pretended not to know him, and even acted disgusted to be in his presence." Desmina gazed up at her again and stated, "Would you have trusted either of them if they had happened to know one another?"

Sarain searched her thoughts and answered, "I suppose not. Besides, then it wouldn't have made sense for James to come to me for help with the story he gave me, if he was already friends with a hunter." "Exactly... The Ancient, he picks the right people to get the job done, he must have saw something in your James that he knew would appeal to you... And he likes to test us... I failed, but you... He's probably still testing you," the beast said hauntingly.

Sarain wondered what her father had planned for her. He wouldn't be pleased to know that his attempt to kill Desmina had failed, and now without James to watch Sarain, his tabs on her would dry up. Would he become disappointed in her as well? Had he planted James to get her to come to his side? Had all of James' actions and feelings just been an act?

Sarain felt violated and helpless. She stood there alone with a beast, and wondered how she could fix the mess she had made of things, and then it hit her. She turned to Desmina and asked, "How strong are your hunting skills?"

A knock came to the door stirring Eddie out of his sleep. He turned and gazed at his clock, the red numbers glowed 1:25am. He grunted at the late hour, and tried to go back to sleep, but the knocks proceeded to come. He then groaned as he got up slowly from his bed. His sheets were tussled from tossing in his sleep, he hadn't been resting well the past couple of nights, and he tangled out of them as he rose up. His bare feet touched the cold tile, and he walked towards the door. Eddie glanced around quickly for a shirt to cover his bare chest, but saw none. He approached the front door to his condo, and peered out the peephole, but it was too dark to see who was knocking. He unlocked the chain first then turned the deadbolt. Finally he turned the doorknob, and the door groaned open.

Eddie squinted sleepily at his caller then his eyes opened wide with surprise.

"What are you doing here?" he abruptly asked.

Chapter 24

Sarain stared back at Eddie, nervously, and muttered out the words, "I need your help." Eddie looked at her with frustration and said, "I told you, I'm through being your consolation prize. If you need help go ask James." Eddie turned to go back inside when Sarain grabbed him by the arm and said, "I need you."

Eddie stopped and turned back around. He stared at Sarain for a moment and then asked, "What is it that you need?" Sarain felt a hint of relief as she answered, "I need you to help me hide someone."

Eddie gave her an annoyed glance as he asked, "It's not James is it?" "No," Sarain immediately replied, "James is gone, and I hope he doesn't come back… This is someone who's help I really need, but I have to keep her safe before anyone else can get to her."

"Her?" Eddie asked curiously, "Who?" Sarain gazed at him with another nervous glance as she replied, "Desmina." His eyes went wide and he quickly remarked, "The beast? Are you crazy?" "She's the only one capable of tracking down an even greater demon, and she's willing to help me do so," Sarain told him while trying to keep him calm. She wanted to tell him the whole truth, about James, about her father, and about herself, but the reaction to her current news went worse than she had expected. Her relationship with Eddie was already on thin ice, she worried that he wouldn't accept the whole truth, and she couldn't bear for him to turn his back on her again.

"Are you sure you can trust her?" Eddie asked with concern. "I know I can for now. We have the same goal, and until we can accomplish it, we need one another's help," she explained. He looked at her curiously and asked, "What do you plan to do?" Sarain stared back into Eddie's brown eyes and answered, "We plan to track a demon called the Ancient, and when we find it, we'll kill it."

Eddie drove Sarain downtown to where she had temporarily stashed Desmina. It was an old molasses factory with a scent so strong that it could mask the demon's own, but it wasn't safe enough. The building was too open, too easily penetrable, and during the day, would let in too much light. Her own place was too predictable, and James and Aion both had easy access to it at this point. Eddie's place was out of the question, she knew he would never agree to it, and she didn't trust Desmina enough to leave her alone with him. Besides, Sarain already knew where she planned to take Desmina, and it was somewhere that could secure her protection; the X. It was a demon haven where she could blend in, and the other demons would mask her scent. Sarain was on good terms with the owners who were demonic vil sangs like Desmina, and she knew she could negotiate a deal with them to help her, since they catered to her already.

Sarain thought of the act of killing her father, and it bothered her, but after all that had happened she knew she couldn't trust him. He was a murderer after all, and nothing could ever justify the carnage that took place the night Sarain lost her clan, not even if she tried, because she knew that Aion had to have been destroying lives long before then. Desmina had even said, she used to kill for him, and he was the one who made her. She wondered how old her father really was to have so much power over demons that he made himself an army, to be able to turn Desmina from a delicate human girl into a massive horrific beast. The turning of humans into demonic vil sangs took many years and a lot of power; it wasn't like a regular vil sang where the humans got infected with the demonic virus. Instead, they would have to feed constantly from other demons, and it would preferably have to be a much stronger demon.

Sarain watched as the streetlights blurred by through the passenger window. The hazy glow of the night began to remind her of the night of the clan attack. She thought of Sephor, and remembered him leading the demon army that night like a general and she wondered if her father made him too. She wondered how long it took for a man to lose his humanity so much that he changed into a monster, and she thought to herself, "Will I change into a creature too or will I be like my father, a wolf in sheep's clothing?"

The sudden jerk of the brakes being stomped down caused Sarain to look up. Eddie was turned towards her waiting, and when she acknowledged him, he asked, "This is the place right?" Sarain glanced out the window and saw the old molasses factory standing before them. She nodded her head, and turned back to Eddie, and said, "It is."

Eddie reached and unhitched his seatbelt, his hand then went for the door handle when Sarain suddenly stopped him by lightly brushing his arm with her hand. He turned to her with confusion to see Sarain staring intently back at him. "Thank you, for everything," she softly told him. Eddie hesitated to respond for a moment, he stared back at her for a while until he finally mustered out, "You're welcome." His response sounded awkward, and it seemed to Sarain that he wanted to say something else, but time was running out, and Sarain needed to get Desmina to the X before sunrise. She opened her door and stepped out. Eddie did the same.

Sarain led the way inside. The abandoned factory was dark with only a little moonlight to light the way. Eddie had trouble seeing and stepping over the debris, and constantly found himself running into it. He wondered why Sarain wasn't having the same problem. Sarain waited in the center of the large service line floor, and after a few moments a large figure emerged from the shadows. Desmina was just as frightening looking as the first time Eddie had seen her, and he found himself trying not to stare at her.

The ride to the X was almost painfully awkward; Desmina sat in back of Eddie's patrol car leaning sideways trying to fit, and Sarain suspected that the beast had never ridden in a car before, and she wondered how she traveled.

Eddie glanced at the creature in his rearview mirror; he looked at the wired screen between him and Desmina and knew that if she wanted, it would do nothing to stop her. When he saw a glint of a lime green eye, he quickly stopped looking.

Sarain watched Eddie, studying him with her peripheral vision, and began to smirk at his awkwardness. Then it occurred to her: his fear of the demonic creature in his backseat could easily transfer to Sarain if he knew the truth about her. She lost her smile, and turned to the window. The thought of Eddie being afraid of her almost made her feel sick, and she began to realize what he had been telling her the night he left; so much could transpire in a look, whether it was love, hate, or fear, one look could change everything.

The car slowed down as Eddie neared the end of Sarain's instructions, and as the car came to a stop, he glanced around with confusion. Sarain turned to him curiously and asked, "What's wrong?" "Where's this building you want to keep her in?" he remarked with puzzlement.

This part of town was surrounded by many rundown buildings, so Sarain could understand his confusion, but at the same time she found it amusing that he couldn't pick out the obvious one that would be called the X. She pointed forward with a laugh, and said, "The X is the one with the big red x spray painted on it."

A few of the buildings had tagging on them, and at first Sarain thought Eddie may have been confused by one of them until she heard him say, "There's no x there, that's just a brick wall." She quickly looked up and saw the same old red x above a large metal door as it had always been, she then turned to Eddie and said, "Are you kidding? It's about a hundred feet right in front of us."

Eddie gave Sarain a baffled glance, and repeated, "That's just a brick wall." Her heart began to race as she stated, "You've picked me up from here dozens of times!" "Yeah, and I thought that it must have been a good hunting ground with there being nothing really around," he said with a note of exclamation in his voice. "You didn't wonder why I was usually dressed up?" Sarain continued to press. "I figured you were being bait," he quickly said.

"But…" Sarain started to say when Desmina shifted in back to lean her way. The car groaned from the sudden weight adjustment, and Sarain felt her side drop closer to the ground. She turned to Desmina whose eyes glowed their unusual shade of lime as she patiently waited for Sarain's attention. She met Desmina's eyes with her own violet ones and when she brought her ear to the wired screen, Desmina hoarsely muttered, "He can't see it." Sarain continued to stare at the beast as she whispered back, "I get that, but I can't understand why."

Desmina struggled to keep her deep strong voice quiet as Eddie stared at them both with confusion and curiosity of what was being exchanged. Desmina continued to explain to Sarain, "Some powerful demons are capable of performing what you would call magic, and two of the most frequent things they can achieve are teleporting and cloaking." Desmina motioned with her eyes towards the building and said, "This place may seem ordinary to you, but it's swimming with energy, the owners must be quite powerful. They've made a glamour so that humans can't see it."

Sarain glanced at Eddie, and knew that there was no simple way to explain what was happening, to him. She looked back to Desmina who quickly stated, "They're not going to let you take him inside, and it's probably better if you didn't."

Sarain's eyes went back to Eddie to see that he was watching her attentively, and she noticed a strange look on his face, a look she had never seen on him before. A look like he wasn't sure if he could trust her.

Chapter 25

Sarain turned to Eddie, and with a solemn look, she said, "This is where we're getting out." Eddie sighed then shrugged with confusion and replied, "Okay." He reached for his door when Sarain suddenly remarked, "No, This is where 'we' are getting out; you're not coming."

Eddie quickly turned back around to face her and immediately said, "No way! There's no chance I'm leaving you alone with that thing; you might trust her, but I certainly do not." He got out of the car, and Sarain followed. She opened the door to the backseat and helped Desmina out. The creature twisted and shifted as she squeezed her way out into the cool night air, and when she stood up fully she towered in stature over the others.

Up close, Desmina was an even more frightful sight, and with this Eddie glanced over at Sarain and sarcastically stated, "And you really think it's safe for me to leave you alone with her?" Sarain answered, "I've already been alone with her tonight," and then she stared at him with an almost cruel intensity and said, "Besides, like you're really capable of protecting me; she knocked you out in seconds the last time you fought; a whole lot of good that'll do me."

A look of shock came over Eddie's face; he hadn't expected Sarain to be so brutally honest to him, but what he didn't know was that the only reason Sarain said what she did was to protect him. Being cruel was the only way Sarain could think of to get Eddie to not follow her. She stared over at him, and spoke in a firm tone, "Go home, Edward."

He stared at her for a moment and then he sighed loudly with frustration, and said, "Yeah, you really needed me…to be your glorified taxi driver," Eddie then shook his head and stated, "And I thought for a second there that you had really changed." He turned his back to Sarain, walked past Desmina, and got back into his car. He drove off quickly; without another word, without asking if Sarain would need a ride back.

Sarain stared at the ground, biting at her bottom lip, holding back the urge to cry. She had hoped to mend things with Eddie, but now she knew she never would, and to her surprise, words of comfort came from an unlikely source.

"You know he's better off," Desmina began to say in her deep hoarse voice, "Not just because those creatures in there would likely kill him, but because he's not like us. He can't understand what it's like to have this darkness burning inside us, and he's better off not being around as that fire grows."

Sarain swung around and glared at Desmina, "You and I are not alike, so don't try and talk to me like we're friends." Sarain then headed towards the club, but Desmina called out to her, "You can try to deny it all you want, and maybe you're not like me now, but someday, you will be."

Sarain didn't answer, she just continued to walk, and Desmina eventually followed without a further word. When she reached the large metal door, Sarain knocked three times, and after a few seconds it opened. The same large vil sang that always guarded the door was the one to open it, he quickly recognized Sarain, and then glanced at Desmina before letting both of them pass. This pale man normally seemed quite enormous, but as Desmina passed him, he looked like a dwarf. He even appeared a bit uneasy as she walked by; it seemed as though not to many demonic vil sangs came to the club, and though the owners were ones as well, the creatures weren't that common.

Sarain led Desmina downstairs to the basement where the owners normally stayed, she had led many vil sangs down there before, but this was the first time that it was for the creature's safety and not for them to be disposed of.

As Sarain descended each step, she started to recall her first time entering the club. She had learned about the place the night before from a scared vil sang that she had only been questioning. They told her that many vil sangs went there and that the club itself was owned by demons that lived in the building. He begged for her to spare him and claimed that he only drank blood he bought from the club, and that he didn't actually kill people. Sarain let him go, more out of pity than anything else, but she knew that if his story didn't check out, she would be tracking him down. The next morning she went to the location he gave her, and sure enough there was a building with a door and a big red X on the bricks. It didn't really look like a club from the outside, but then its clientele needed to stay low profile.

Without thinking or worry, she tried opening the large metal door. Of course it was locked, but after beating the lock with a brick lying on the ground, Sarain was soon walking into the darkened building. Immediately she saw the vast club room, and though there were no windows, she could see well enough to know that the floor was empty. She found the door leading to the basement after that, and made the same journey down those stone spiraling steps as she was doing now. It was at the bottom that she found two demonic vil sangs waiting for her, both large in size, both having been awakened when she broke in. But instead of attacking her immediately, they offered to strike up a deal with her. This caught Sarain by surprise, but apparently they had learned of her through demons who had managed to escape her blade. Though at first she was cautious, she realized this was in her best interest; fighting two demonic vil sangs on her own wasn't a safe move.

At the time, Sarain had thought that these demons were just as secretly afraid of her as she was of them, but now as she neared the last step, she realized that maybe they trusted her because they knew she had seen through their glamour to keep humans out. Had they realized the whole time that she was more than human? Thinking of this made Sarain uneasy, and she doubted her alliance with these beasts, but felt since Desmina was one of their own she figured at least she would be safe here.

Sarain stepped down onto the concrete floor where once again the owners were already waiting. She stepped forward as Desmina stepped down into the room, and approached the owners saying, "This is a 'friend' of mine," she almost choked on the word, but continued, "She's being hunted by someone, and I need to secure her safety. Can I keep her here?"

The creatures both turned and looked at each other, and without exchanging a word between them they replied, "Any friend of yours is safe with us." Sarain had a feeling that this only extended to friends with demonic blood, but that was all she needed for now. She turned to Desmina and asked her, "Do you feel safe staying here?" The creature glanced down at her and answered, "Anyone who can cloak a place like this is strong enough to keep "him" at bay."

Sarain then nodded in agreement, and turned to leave, but before she could ascend the first step, Desmina stopped her by saying, "Don't trust him," Sarain turned back around to meet Desmina's stare as she added, "He's smart, and knows exactly where to attack you... He's good at twisting things to sound true." Sarain thought of what he had told her about her grandfather and wondered if he killing her mother had all been a lie. She glanced at Desmina again, and wondered what it was that Aion had said to her that made her first trust him.

Sarain turned back around, and began her trek back up the spiraling staircase.

Sleep didn't come easy to Sarain, not only was the sun rising by the time she got home, letting in lots of light into her bedroom, but the many thoughts circling in her mind kept her from relaxing. She thought of Eddie, worrying about what he must think of her, and she thought about her grandfather, and wondered if the stern man really had it in him to poison his daughter. She didn't want to believe Aion, but Sarain also contemplated over the fact that he had told her that black mirrors only let someone talk to people in purgatory. Even if it was a lie, why hadn't she seen her mother, or Orran, or even Kit in the mirror? She only ever saw Delmar.

Sarain finally fell asleep after a long while, and her anxious nerves caused her to dream of disturbing things. She dreamt of monsters, demons, and any creature that could strike fear in someone's heart. She dreamt of the clan attack all over again, but this time it was different. This time she didn't see her memories, but instead her fears. She watched from her hiding spot as Sephor approached the blade-wielding Orran. She watched as her friend swung at the beast and struck him in the arm. Then she saw the beast strike back at Orran and slice him across the chest. It was then that Sarain made her grave mistake, she gasped, causing Orran to look in her direction. And once again Sephor grabbed him by the throat and bite him. But when the beast let go, and let her friend's body drop to the ground, it was no longer Sephor who stood before her. Instead she saw herself as she was now, a grown adult, but with something wrong with her face. Her eyes glowed a bright violet, her teeth had fangs, and her skin had turned hard and gray. She wiped Orran's blood from her mouth as she stared down at his lifeless body, and though Sarain knew this was just a dream, she felt that in a way it was true, she might as well have killed Orran herself, and that one day she may even be a beast that could truly do such a thing.

The dream stirred Sarain, but she didn't wake; instead she went deeper into her mind and saw her other fear. She watched herself as a small child playing with a doll outside her mother's door. Delmar had been in his daughter's room for some time, and when he finally emerged he had a strange look about his face. It wasn't a look of sadness, but more an expressionless appearance. His demeanor seemed blank like he had been removed of emotion; he wasn't angry or sad, he just was.

When he approached Sarain slowly, she put down her doll, and stared up at her grandfather. Tears already began to form in her eyes, and she knew unlike any other five year old should know, exactly what her grandfather prepared to tell her. Her mother was dead. The words seemed flat as they came out his mouth, they felt lifeless. She's dead.

Sarain buried her head and tears into her doll as she wailed out in grief. Her screams reached that pitch that only a child can. That's when Delmar leaned down towards his grandchild, he reached out for her, but instead of taking the child into his arms, he grabbed for her doll. He tugged the doll out on her hands and firmly said, "Stop crying!" But Sarain could not; she continued to sob as she stared up at her grandfather, and then he repeated more loudly, "Stop crying!"

Sarain defied her grandfather and continued to cry; she had lost her mother, and was too heartbroken to fear her grandfather. Delmar stared down at her for a moment longer, then threw down the doll and muttered, "You make me sick." He left the room after that, and it brought some relief to little Sarain.

Sarain watched herself as a child, continuing to cry, and she wished she could comfort that child, but no one would. This wasn't a dream, but how it really went.

When Sarain woke up that afternoon, she was in tears and still tired. Her memories of Delmar didn't help her believe in his innocence, and the only thing she could think to do would be to ask him herself. She went to her kitchen table where she had last left the cracked black mirror and stared down into its dark glass. Delmar didn't always appear to her when she wanted him to, and their last conversion didn't end pleasantly, but still she had to try and reach him.

Sarain carefully picked up the mirror, trying not to further damage the broken glass and called out her grandfather's name into it. "Delmar, grandfather," she repeated over and over at it, but nothing appeared in the mirror. Her frustrations began to grow and her grip tightened on the frame, "Delmar, show yourself!" But he didn't appear.

Sarain placed the mirror back down, and started to walk away from it, when a sick feeling growing in the pit of her stomach caused her to glance back at the mirror. It still remained blank, but Sarain once again grabbed at its frame and lifted the mirror to her face. She saw only her own reflection, but this time while staring into its glass she found the nerve to cry out, "Damn it, Delmar, did you kill my mother?"

Within seconds her own image began to cloud, and her grandfather's face appeared. He stared back at his granddaughter, as she asked again, "Did you murder my mother?"

He didn't answer right away and instead asked, "Did your father tell you this?" Sarain stared into the glass and replied, "Aion did, but I don't know if I can trust him. I need to hear you say it. Did you murder her? Are you in purgatory?"

Delmar looked away, and a look of fear came upon his face, and Sarain knew what he was about to say. "Yes, I am in purgatory, because I did murder Ariana."

Sarain had wanted so much for it not to be true, she wanted Aion to be a liar, and for him to be the only villain in this story. But the look on her grandfather's face was clear; he had done exactly what he had said.

A tear escaped her eyes as she asked her grandfather, "Why?" And he began to cry, "Your mother never wanted you to become a hunter, she wanted to leave the clan with you. But I couldn't let her do that; she would have gone to him. He would have found the both of you."

"So you killed her?" Sarain cried, "You poisoned your own daughter? All that time?" "You don't understand," Delmar proclaimed with a look of panic still on his face, "She chose that demon once before, she would have done it again... I already lost my daughter to evil. I wasn't going to let her take you."

Sarain's heart nearly stopped as she realized that her grandfather killed his own daughter for her. She had always felt as though he hated her for being what she was, but now she started to feel as though the reason he hated her wasn't out of disgust, but because he had loved her so much that he murdered his own daughter in order to protect her.

Sarain gasped as she struggled to stammer out, "You don't know that she would have gone to him... My mother was a good woman." Delmar tried to plead to her, "No, she would have brought you to him. Her love for that creature blinded her." "That's not true, my mother loved me!" she shouted into the mirror.

Delmar started to explain himself again, but Sarain stopped him by yelling, "Shut up! Don't you realize it's all your fault?" His eyes and mouth stood open, but he did not interrupt while Sarain said, "He had you and all of our clan killed because of what you did!" Delmar was silent; he didn't try to defend himself, and it was his silence that bothered Sarain most of all, because she realized he wasn't sorry.

She held the mirror's frame tightly as she stared at her grandfather and quietly whispered, "You ruined my life." Then she felt herself let go. The mirror slipped from her hands and hit the table; it shattered into pieces that fell from its frame. The dark shards bounced off and onto the floor, and it took Sarain a moment to realize that she was now alone. She had broken the black mirror for good and her grandfather would not be coming back. She didn't know if she was relieved to be rid of him or disappointed that she could never make him repent for what he had done. What she did know was that she came from a family of murderers, and it was only a matter of time before the demon blood in her veins would bubble to the surface.

Sarain stared down at one of the larger shards of glass, and thought about how sharp it looked.

Chapter 26

Desmina sat on the cold hard floor of one of the basement's small rooms. She sat staring at her hands, and she tried to picture what her hands used to look like. They had been gray, scaly, and clawed over for so long. She couldn't remember what shade of skin she once had; she had only looked human for such a small fraction of her life. Her body had grown so large and fierce, and she tried to think how it felt to be found beautiful.

Cyrus was the only thing that reminded her of being human, even though he had become just as much a monster as herself. She could still remember her brother as a man; he had had fair skin, sandy blond hair, and olive green eyes just like hers had once been. They were twins and their resemblance was uncanny, and was even so as they grew into monsters. Aion had lured them both in with foolish fantasies of eternal youth and beauty, but it wasn't long after their blood had become infected that that dream turned into a harsh reality, and only Aion's looks stayed the same. They stuck with the Ancient out of fear, doing everything he asked of them. He hovered near them always, making sure they wouldn't gain a streak of independence, and the only time he left their sides was when he would parade as a man amongst humans.

Desmina thought of the last time Aion returned after one of his excursions, the last one before she parted ways with him. He had seemed different, quieter, meaner, and she couldn't understand why. He had started beating Cyrus after only a moment of delay on one of his requests, and Desmina watched as her brother became bloody and near death with fear of punishment for stepping out of line herself if she tried to help her brother. Aion was never the same after that, and though he had always been cruel up until then, he had always seemed fueled by greed, but after that last excursion, that greed appeared to have dissipated into emptiness.

Desmina tried to count the years since then, but couldn't get an exact number. It was somewhere at twenty odd years ago. Then she thought of Sarain, she looked to be in her twenties, and wondered if that last excursion was when Aion met her mother. Aion never talked about his trips, and could have done anything in the process, but Desmina wondered what it was about that last one that changed his demeanor.

A creak of the door to her room opening caused Desmina to look up. She half expected to see one of the owners checking in on her, but she knew that demonic vil sangs like herself didn't get tied up in worrying about other's comfort. The other half of her knew who it was behind that door, and had been expecting him all the while. She looked up to see her former master walk into the room, his violet eyes glaring down at her.

"I knew you would come," Desmina muttered out softly, almost sounding feminine. Aion stared down at his once protégé as he closed the door behind him. Desmina glanced away from his burning gaze, and she thought of how it felt when the wind blew through her once long blond hair.

Eddie drove home that evening after a long day shift of patrolling the streets. He felt frustrated and exhausted after hardly getting any sleep from Sarain's late visit. All day long he thought of how she had used him for mere transportation, duping him once again into helping her. He was tired of the drama that came with dating Sarain, though he thought how "dating" was not the right word to use to describe his relationship with her, because Sarain never let him in enough or around her enough for him to actually date her. They didn't go to restaurants, or movies, and she had never once met a friend of his. Their time consisted in hunting creatures, and sex that resulted in her leaving immediately after he would fall asleep; she refused to stay the night at his place.

Eddie had spent two years of his life trying to get to know Sarain, and still she was a mystery to him. A part of him hoped to never see her again, wanting to avoid further pain of rejection, but a part of him also needed closure. Whether or not Eddie wanted to admit it, Sarain was the love of his life, and he knew the only way he could get over her was with closure; he would have to finally turn her away and tell her no more.

Eddie parked his car down the street of his condo, and put money in his meter. He then walked towards the steps to his place, and as he approached he noticed a figure slumped by his door. He placed his hand on the gun at his side, and waited to see if the figure was a homeless man, which did frequent his area, or perhaps a creature that had tracked his scent back to his home; Sarain often warned him of this happening. The little light that the streetlights provided showed him that the figure wasn't large, but he still couldn't make out who it was; he would have to go in for a closer look.

Eddie started up his stairs, still cautious, and as his foot landed on the second step, the figure shifted and a head popped up. A pair of familiar eyes stared back at him, and he soon realized that it was Sarain. The first thought that came to his mind was, "No, you have to leave," but as he opened his mouth to tell her so, he noticed the streetlight reflecting off her dampened face, she was crying. He then wondered how long she had been waiting there for him.

Eddie's face softened as he moved his hand off his gun. He reached down to help Sarain up as he asked her, "What's wrong?"

As usual, Sarain did not say, but unlike herself, when she finally stood up, she didn't brush herself off or refuse his help, or even back away. No, instead she quickly embraced Eddie, wrapping her arms tightly around him, and buried her face against his chest. Eddie was stunned, he wasn't used to Sarain being so emotional, and never knew her to need him in such a way. He placed his hands on her back, and held her to him. He could feel her still crying, her body lightly shuttering with each tear, and he was amazed how small and frail Sarain felt. Eddie had never seen her as a helpless creature, not even after seeing her take a beating in battle, because even then she still was a fighter, but now more than ever he saw her as a woman, just as delicate as any other, and just as capable of having her heart broken.

Eddie held Sarain there in the darkness, outside his door, for a while in silence. When her crying finally slowed down and began to stop, he whispered to her, "Are you alright? Do you want to go inside?" He looked down at Sarain to see her puffy violet eyes staring up at him, and she nodded her head softly in agreement. Then she did something else that surprised him, she weakly asked, "Can I stay the night?"

It took Eddie only a second to answer, "Of course."

Eddie held Sarain that night. They didn't talk, and he didn't press the issue of what was bothering her. He simply watched Sarain as she fell asleep and knew that if she was able to finally come this far, she would eventually tell him on her own time, and he was willing to wait. Sarain fell asleep quickly in his arms, and he laid there listening to her breathe. She was finally letting him take care of her, and she had even come to him.

As Eddie laid there with Sarain in his arms, he never felt more at peace, yet at the same time a sinking feeling in the pit of his stomach made him worry that he would lose her. At that moment, he swore to himself that he would never let anyone take her away again.

Sarain woke up to an empty bed. She lifted her head and glanced quickly around the room. Eddie was not in sight. She slowly rose from the bed, while wondering if he had to work. She glanced at the picture of Eddie's parents on his nightstand, and wondered what it was like for him growing up with a mother and father, given they were gone now, but it must have been nice having both of them for as long as he had.

Sarain gave another quick glance around the room; there were no pictures of her in it, mostly because she didn't like to take pictures. There was no real particular reason for it; she didn't see anything in pictures like she did mirrors; she just didn't like to see herself in general. She wasn't sure what exactly it was that she didn't like about herself, she honestly couldn't tell if she was attractive or not, she just wasn't used to seeing what she looked like. After spending so much time avoiding mirrors, she had trouble recognizing herself when the opportunity arose. But taking a photograph seemed like something Eddie would want to do, so Sarain figured that one day she should.

Sarain walked to the bedroom door, and as she opened it she was immediately flooded with the rich scent of food. The scent led her to the kitchen where she found Eddie cooking up a storm. He looked up as she stepped into the room, and he gave her a smile. "Go ahead and sit down," he said motioning her to the table, "It's almost ready."

Sarain sat and stretched as she asked, "You don't have work?" "I took the day off," Eddie replied, "I thought we could use the time together." The response slightly surprised Sarain, but she knew Eddie was a caring man, and very few people had ever shown her such kindness.

Eddie placed a plate full of eggs, bacon, sausage, and hash browns down in front of Sarain, and she stared at it in amazement. "What's wrong?" he asked curiously. "Nothing, I'm just not used to having so much food," Sarain remarked. She usually rationed her meals, and ate only what she needed to provide her strength and energy, she didn't eat for enjoyment.

Eddie sat down next to Sarain with his own plate full of food and commented, "No wonder you're so skinny. It looks like I should cook for you more often." They ate without much more said, and by the end Sarain was forcing herself to eat the last link of sausage on her plate. She didn't like to waste food, and figured it was the least she could do after Eddie had gone through the trouble of preparing her food.

Sarain began to get up to take care of her plate when Eddie took it out from under her and said, "You're my guest, I won't have you cleaning." She sat there awkwardly waiting as Eddie washed their plates, and as he cleaned, she noticed how happy he seemed. It was just a simple task, but it seemed that the fact that Sarain was there, and that it was her dish he was washing made him pleased.

Eddie turned off the water and turned to Sarain. He looked happy, and though Sarain wasn't used to expressing it, she felt happy too. Eddie then approached Sarain, his smile quickly changed to a serious expression, and she began to worry about what was crossing his mind.

"There's something I've been wanting to ask you," Eddie suddenly said in a solemn tone. Sarain wondered if something was wrong, if Eddie was still having doubts about her; if the past was catching up to them once again. "I don't know if this is the right time to bring this up, but..." he began to trail off, and for a moment Sarain looked away in fear. When she brought her eyes back to him, she noticed that he had taken something out from his pocket, and after a soft click echoed out through the air, Sarain immediately realized why Eddie's demeanor had changed.

She watched as he bent down on one knee and raised the small velvety box towards her. Inside it was a small silvery ring, simple and with a single diamond on the band. Sarain hadn't expected this, and given that their relationship had been rocky recently, she wondered how long he had had this ring, waiting to propose.

"I've been wanting for a while now to say this. Sarain, I love you. I love you more than I thought I could ever love someone, and when I think about my future, all I see is you," Eddie stated. Sarain's heart raced as she looked at the ring then at Eddie, and though she felt as though she were going to explode, she waited quietly and calmly for him to finish. "I want to spend the rest of my life with you, I want to grow old with you, have children with you. And I want to start my life with you now. So Sarain, will you marry me?" Eddie asked finally, sounding heartfelt and excited.

Sarain looked down into Eddie's eager eyes, and though she almost felt herself reaching for the ring, she hesitated. And she realized that all she really heard was

240

that he wanted to have children with her, and Sarain knew that wasn't a possibility, her body was barely managing to fight off the demon blood inside of her, she couldn't possibly have a child. Then the words "grow old with you" rang out in her ears, and Sarain realized that that too may not be a possibility, she could turn more demonic at any time, and maybe even stop aging like a vil sang.

Sarain knew she had to tell Eddie the truth about herself, but as she looked down into his eyes, she found herself unable to say the words, and instead what came out was, "I can't."

Eddie stared up at Sarain in disbelief, his face looked vacant of expression, and he remained there for a while, trying to figure out what had just happened. He didn't react, he just closed the ring box and asked, "You can't right now?"

"I can't ever," Sarain muttered, surprising even herself. She knew that if she just told Eddie the truth that he would understand, but a part of her remained holding back. She would rather have him hate her as a human, than see her as a demon, and it was with that thought that made Sarain stand up and say, "I'm sorry Edward... But I'm planning on leaving soon." It was a thought that had been crossing Sarain's mind for a while, "The number of demons here has been dwindling, and it's time for me to move on."

"I could go with you," Eddie quickly said. It almost made Sarain smile, but she forced herself to say, "No, your life is here; your job, your friends. I usually move more frequently than this... I stayed here too long, and now there's nothing left for me."

Eddie gave her a look of frustration and suddenly stated, "What about us? Aren't I enough to change your 'routine'?" It was a question Sarain had hoped he wouldn't ask, and though she truly cared for him, the honest answer was, "No." Her mission was too important for her to let herself go astray, and she knew that Eddie was better off with her not in his life, even if she wasn't.

Her answer rang out in Eddie's ears like a harsh noise, "No." She gave no explanation and said it without feeling. And as Eddie began to get up from his embarrassing position, he threw down the ring box, and immediately went to anger. "Why did you even come here?" he said it full of hate while glaring into Sarain's eyes, "You act like you want me, you say that you need me, and now suddenly you're leaving? Are you trying to make me hate you? Because coming here and telling me this is worse than if you had just disappeared!"

Sarain didn't respond, she simply stood there with a trembling Eddie, not looking him in the eye, and it only made him madder. "You won't even look at me! At least the old distant Sarain I knew had the nerve to look me in the eye... I don't know what's going on with you, but I know you're lying to me," Eddie remarked to her. Sarain hadn't realized how much of herself she had let him see, but even with this in mind, she offered Eddie no explanation.

He stood there for a moment, waiting, hoping for something from Sarain, but she didn't budge. So finally, Eddie pointed towards the door and told her, "Get out!"

She didn't hesitate on his request; she quickly turned away and left the room. She left quietly, not even slamming the door behind her, but this only further infuriated Eddie, because it meant that Sarain didn't care enough to get upset with him. But what he couldn't see was the emotions that were welling up inside of her or the tears that escaped her eyes just as she closed his door.

After a minute to compose himself, Eddie bent down and picked up the ring box, but the moment his fingers touched its velvet his fury came back. He threw the box across the room and cried out with aggravation. And just as he began to let his anger take over, it suddenly stopped when a soft knock came to his door. It was still early, too early for visitors, and with Sarain just barely having left, he realized that she must have come to her senses; she had come back to him.

Eddie rushed to the door and quickly opened it, wanting to take Sarain into his arms. The bright light of early morning came rushing in, and the first thing he saw was a pair of violet eyes, but it took only a second for him to realize that these weren't the same pair that he often stared lovingly into. In fact, these eyes had no love for Eddie.

Chapter 27

Sarain spent most of the day walking around town. She knew the city well, too well, that it felt time to leave. She was tired of hurting Eddie, and she knew that if she stayed, she would only hurt him further. The only thing keeping her from leaving that very instant was Aion; she needed to resolve things with her father. Sarain knew that Desmina was depending on her for both protection and to take down Aion, but the more Sarain thought about it, the more she wasn't sure if she could kill her father. Though he had been a stranger for most of her life, and his crimes were horrible, he was still her father. The blood they shared wouldn't change even if Sarain killed him, but running wouldn't make it go away either. She wanted to go about her life as she had done before; no strings tied to anyone, and nothing but her mission to drive her.

It was about an hour until dusk, and Sarain felt it was a good time to check on Desmina, before the club would get busy with customers. She would help her get out of town if that was what Desmina wished, but that was all Sarain was willing to do for her. Desmina was a killer after all. Aion may have been the one giving the orders, but she had chosen to follow them. As for the club, Sarain didn't know if the owners were trust worthy enough to keep humans off the menu with her not around, part of her almost didn't care, but the hunter in her was devising a plan.

When Sarain arrived at the X, the door was locked, but with Sarain's ever growing strength, she still managed to let herself in. She walked down to the basement, taking her time down its long stairwell. The basement was dark as usual, but Sarain's eyes adjusted so quickly that it didn't filter in as a problem. She searched around for Desmina; Sarain knew that the owners were lurking somewhere in the basement as well, but she didn't worry. Sarain didn't fear these creatures, but not out of trust, in fact the more she thought of them the more she didn't trust them. The fact that they had let her walk away that first day said more to her than she could have initially fathomed. They had to have suspected what she was after knowing she had seen past their glamour, and their partnership with her may have been a way to lure her to their side.

The main room was empty, but the stench that always clung to the air seemed stronger. Sarain wondered if all her senses were getting stronger. She glanced at the large metal contraption that stood in the room; the grinders. Many demons and vil sangs had met their fate inside that device, and just looking at it made Sarain feel sick. Though, as she approached it, she felt herself being drawn in for a closer look. The harsh metal blades looked dirty and tarnished as they always did. Such thick metal being stored underground should be cool to the touch, but as Sarain brought her hand to one of its sharp blades, she noticed that it felt warm, and that its grime was still sticky; the sludge felt fresh.

Sarain was immediately hit with a revelation, and she instantly called out Desmina's name. Within moments the owners entered the room, and one of the demonic giants reported to Sarain that Desmina had gone on her own accord shortly after Sarain had left. Sarain knew this was impossible, because she had left her just before sunrise, and no demon would chance the sun just to find a different hiding place.

"You're lying," Sarain stated firmly, as she continued to search around the basement, but she knew that if these creatures wanted to make Desmina disappear, they could. Sarain felt herself growing frustrated, but held back her emotions as she turned back to these creatures. But with a swift turn of her head and a glint in her eye, Sarain knew the owners saw what Sarain had felt; for a fraction of a second, her eyes had glowed. She didn't say anything as she stood there across from the creatures, and they were the ones to break the silence.

"You won't find her," one of the demons spoke then the other picked up in almost the same voice saying, "He doesn't want her found."

Sarain stared at the owners for a moment until she finally remarked, "You serve the Ancient." "As should you," they both said in unison. Sarain felt herself begin to tremble with anger, as she realized exactly why these creatures had trusted her. She stared up at them with the eyes she knew they had recognized long ago and asked, "Why bow down to him?"

"He made us what we are today," one demon replied, then the other added, "And he blessed our home with safety." That was the moment Sarain realized that the X wasn't cloaked by the owners, Aion had made the glamour. He had sold his soul for power, the power that allowed him to cross barriers, build armies, and walk in sunlight, also allowed him to cloak demon's homes from humans' view. Her father's power extended further than she had realized, Sarain knew now there was no escaping his watchful eye.

"I will never serve my father," Sarain told the beasts. The two creatures exchanged glances then turned back to Sarain, and stated, "Then you are no longer welcome here."

Sarain stared at the large beasts, and didn't say another word. She simply turned around and walked back up the stairs. She wasn't in a position to take on two demonic vil sangs at once, but she also wasn't going to let them continue with what they were doing. Their word of trust had been the only thing keeping her from acting on her natural instincts; now that that was gone, Sarain would no longer be holding back. The X and its owners' time were nearing their end.

Sarain finally made her way back to her own door. She opened it and stepped inside, but as she crossed her threshold, she noticed the place no longer felt like home. Broken glass still lay scattered on and around her table, the rooms felt empty and lifeless, and the air seemed stale. It was time to go, and everything around her was telling her so. Sarain went to her bedroom, and went straight for her closet. She pulled out a suitcase to begin packing up her things, and as she went to place it on her bed, she suddenly stopped, as she took notice of something she had not seen before. Lying on her pillow was the photograph of her and her mother, the same one that Aion had taken when he had broken into and raided her place. It sat there with the image facing up as if it had never left. Nothing else was out of place and the door had even been locked when Sarain had entered her home, it was as if Aion had suddenly appeared in her home only to leave what he had stolen from her, with only the photograph as proof.

Sarain stood there stunned as she stared at her mother's image, wondering why Aion would have gone through the trouble to steal the picture only to return it later. She reached down slowly and took hold of the photograph. As she brought it closer to her, she immediately dropped it when she noticed what it had been covering. Also on her pillow, hiding underneath the photo, was a shiny silvery ring, the same that Eddie had tried to give Sarain earlier.

Sarain's hand went to her mouth as she began to gag. Her stomach quickly went sour from fear as she realized that Aion had Eddie. She looked away from the ring with tears forming in her eyes, and her eyes then settled back on her mother's photograph. The picture had flipped and written on the back was, "Meet me at the molasses factory." Sarain realized that Aion was talking about the place she temporarily hid Desmina a couple nights earlier; he must have tracked her scent there.

Sarain knew she had to go see her father; she couldn't avoid it, not if she ever wanted to see Eddie again and have him be safe. Her worst fears were coming true. She had endangered Eddie's life, but as she looked down at the ring, she swore to herself that she would not lose him like she lost Kit. Whatever she had to do to protect him, she would, even if that meant killing her father.

The sky had turned dark by the time Sarain finally reached the molasses factory. Clouds filled the sky hiding the stars and blocking out the light of the moon. She stared up at the large abandoned building, as she stood in its looming shadow, and as she gazed up at it she only felt fear growing inside her. She had faced many battles, but there was no preparing herself for this one. She stood there, scared and alone, and the only person she would call on for help was waiting somewhere inside and in need of her.

As Sarain hesitated to go inside, she felt how tired she was of always sacrificing her happiness; she had lost so much time, so many people, and so much energy in her life of hunting. Before she finally moved forward, Sarain's last thought was that this was the last time, the last battle. She would start to live her life for herself, and her vengeance would be over. She wanted to be happy, even if that meant giving up the life she had always known, and settling down with Eddie.

The door to the factory hung open, barely on its hinges. Sarain stepped in, not worried about stealth. After all, she was expected. She walked over and passed the clutter, and made her way to the heart of the building, and there in the large open floor room, stood Aion with Eddie. Eddie's hands appeared tied and Aion had forced him down onto his knees with a sword to his back. Sarain gripped her machete tightly, as she slowly approached her father, and with another step, Aion called out, "That's close enough."

Sarain stopped immediately and quickly stated, "Let him go!" "You know I can't, not unless you agree to come with me," Aion told his daughter. Sarain glared over at her father, and heartlessly said, "Anything, just let him go." Aion stared at his daughter curiously, and replied, "I don't think you mean that," he then glanced at the machete she clutched in her hand and remarked, "It looks like you've come here to kill me."

Aion gave a quick glance down at Eddie then back to his daughter as he said, "Are you really willing to murder your own father to save this weak creature?" Sarain stared at Aion as she responded, "There's a lot I'm willing to do these days; killing you to save him really isn't a big issue for me."

Aion smiled at his daughter, and simply stated, "You're more like me than you think." He then looked to Eddie once again and asked, "Do you really think he'll still love you after he knows what you are?"

Sarain's heart pounded in her chest, she didn't know the answer to that question, she wasn't even sure if Eddie would still want her after all she had put him through. Then as though reading her thoughts, she heard Eddie say, "Of course I'll still love her; even with her father being a psychopath!"

Aion glanced back down at Eddie and he kicked him in the back, stating, "That question wasn't for you!" He looked back to Sarain and remarked, "Besides, you don't know what my daughter truly is…" Sarain glared at her father and immediately stated, "Don't you dare," in a deep and angry tone. But Aion merely smiled at the annoyance of his daughter, and continued, "She's like me, more than human, and eventually she'll be one of those creatures you hunt."

"Don't listen to him!" Sarain called out to Eddie, as her heart continued to race. "Don't believe me?" Aion started to say, "Then look at her eyes." Sarain knew her violet eyes gave her away as something not quite normal, but as she saw the look on Eddie's face as he stared up at her, she knew that this time her eyes said something more than what they usually spoke to him. This time with her emotions running high and her heart racing, she felt what Eddie saw; her eyes were glowing, and in the poorly lit factory, there would be no missing this source of light.

Chapter 28

Eddie gazed up at Sarain in shock, his brown eyes wide with bewilderment. His mouth gaped open, but no sound came out. The stunned look on his face was almost enough to stop Sarain's heart. For a moment, the factory stood in silence; it was only a mere moment, but it felt like an eternity to Sarain.

A smile spread across Aion's face as he saw the fear radiating from his daughter's eyes. "Now do you see, my child, he and all the others like him, will never accept you for what you are. You are better off with me," he said smugly.

Sarain looked to her father, and couldn't tell if he was acting in cruelness or in love for his daughter, and for a second, Sarain understood why he so desperately wanted her to join him. As she stared into her father's eyes, she saw herself in them, she saw her in him, and Sarain thought of going with Aion.

Eddie continued to stare up at the woman he loved, disbelief still on his face. His eyes followed Sarain's, and as he studied her contemplative expression, he soon realized what she was thinking. "No Sarain!" he quickly yelled out, "Don't go with him!"

She turned to Eddie, surprised by his outburst. Her eyes locked on to his, and when they did, the glowing dissipated. He gazed up at her lovingly and called out, "Don't leave. It doesn't matter what you are, just that you're the woman I fell in love with." Sarain felt her heart skip a beat, and she started to smile. "I still love you, Sarain. I will always love you," Eddie told her.

"I…," Sarain began to say when the sudden movements of her father caught her attention. Her eyes went to the gleam on Aion's blade. It happened in a fraction of a second; there was no stopping him. She saw his blade quickly move back into the air, and then he thrust it square into the center of Eddie's back. Eddie's eyes went wide; he tried to take a breath, but appeared to choke. His eyes stared up at Sarain until they lost focus. Sarain watched in horror as the blade went straight through, and stuck out of Eddie's chest. Aion put a foot on his back then pushed on him until his sword came out. Eddie's body fell face first to the ground, barely making a thud.

"E...D...D...I...E...!" Sarain screamed out.

She dropped to her knees; she had failed, she had failed Eddie. Tears streamed down her face as she stared at his lifeless body. She couldn't bear to lose Eddie; she needed him. She screamed in agony as her pain began to take form; a fire within her grew and its flame reflected in her eyes. They glowed as brightly as any creature she had ever fought. She could feel the demonic blood burning inside her now, there was no doubt: she was a beast herself, just in human form. Her skin burned and her muscles throbbed; her rage and sorrow was forcing its way out. She could feel her teeth beginning to grow, and she knew now that she had fangs; just like a vil sang, they came out when she became enraged.

Sarain's fiery eyes rose up slowly from her lover's body, and settled on his killer. She glared at her father, as she tightened her grip on the machete. Without another second of hesitation she ran at Aion, her blade raised high. She swung at her father, perfectly, but in less than a blink of an eye, he had moved. Before Sarain could turn to find him, Aion grabbed both of her arms and pulled them back behind her, forcing her to drop her blade. Pain shot through her shoulders as he dislocated both of them while holding her back.

Sarain hollered in anger, and shouted; "Now you're going to kill me too?" Aion moved his lips near his daughter's ear and muttered, "The plan was never to kill you. I just didn't want you with that mortal."

"You hated him that much?" Sarain cried out in confusion. "It's not a matter of hate, my child. I didn't hate the man for who he was, he just wasn't worthy of you. None of them are," Aion spoke soothingly to her, "Mortals are weak; they easily break, and they die. They always die. Learn this, and it'll spare you future pain."

"Are you crazy?" Sarain shouted, "Future pain? I'm always in pain! And you just foresaw to it that I stay that way! Just because you're a demon, doesn't mean you won't die. You can die, and I'm going to see to it that you do!"

Aion quickly turned Sarain to face him, his inhuman strength made sure she couldn't move as he firmly told her, "You will join me one day!" Sarain spat on her father, making him tighten his grip on her even more. His fingers dug into her skin causing her to bruise and bleed. His luminescent eyes burned down into Sarain's as he shouted, "You may have gotten away from me once before Ariana, but I will not let you leave again!"

Sarain's expression went from anger to shock as she responded, "I am not my mother!" Suddenly, Aion's eyes lost focus as he his own expression went blank; he then looked back at his daughter, and said, "It doesn't matter. I won't let you ruin your life carrying on the way you have been. You will join me someday, even if I have to break you to do so."

Sarain stared up at her father in horror, and all she could muster out was, "What gives you the right?" Aion gazed into her eyes and replied, "Because I am your father, and you're the only child I'll ever have. The fact that you even exist is miraculous, and a power like that should only be mine."

"I am not yours," Sarain cried. Aion then leaned down to his daughter, his cold breath on her skin and simply said, "Yes you are." He then shoved her back with great force, and Sarain fell back until she hit the ground. Her head bounced against the concrete, and things went black.

Sarain opened her eyes and immediately felt the throbbing in her head and arms. Her jaw clenched up from the unbearable pain, and she then realized that her fangs had retracted. Sarain sat up with a wave of dizziness as she tried to remember where she was. She wasn't sure how much time had gone by, but she was surrounded by darkness, and she thought she was alone. Then Sarain turned her head, and she saw Eddie's body lying in a pool of blood, and then she remembered everything.

Tears began to fall from Sarain's eyes as she struggled to crawl to Eddie. Pain shot through her arms as she dragged herself to him. She touched his hand first and it was cold. As she moved closer she felt his blood beginning to soak into her pants, and that too felt cold. Sarain trembled as she stared down at Eddie; he laid face down, and she longed to see his face once more. She placed her hand on his shoulder and then strained to turn him over. Eddie's body made a swish noise as he slide in his own blood, the sound made Sarain so sick to her stomach that she had to swallow down her vomit.

She gazed down at Eddie and then let out a short yelp; his eyes still remained open and his face was cover with his blood. His eyes were glassy and lifeless; staring down at him he no longer looked like the man she knew. Eddie was gone, and all that was left was a shell. Sarain brought her hands to her face to wipe her eyes, and then stopped when she saw that they were covered with Eddie's blood. She cried out in agony, and knew that she could never wash away the pain of Eddie's death. She blamed herself for letting him into her life, she should have known better; everyone around her always dies.

Then Aion suddenly popped into Sarain's mind, and she immediately started looking around the room, but it was of no use, he was long gone. Sarain wondered if her father would be coming back for her, and she prayed that he wouldn't. Sarain wanted so much to kill Aion, but knew she wasn't ready; he had bested her so quickly and effortlessly that she knew she wasn't strong enough just yet. She remembered him swearing to make her join him, which meant he planned to come for her again, and Sarain realized that she had to run. She couldn't face Aion again, not until she was ready for him, she couldn't let him break her.

Sarain gazed down once again at Eddie, and ran her fingers slowly over his face. She closed his eyes, and then pretended he was only sleeping. So many times she used to watch him sleep, she just wanted to do so one last time. She leaned down and kissed him on his forehead then whispered, "Goodnight."

Sarain then left Eddie to sleep.

It was late into the night after Sarain left the molasses factory, but she wasn't ready to go home. She walked the streets, sticky with blood, but with a purpose. She went after hours shopping downtown at a few hardware and supplies stores until she found what she needed. Windows, bars, and alarms did nothing to stop her as she gathered the ingredients an old friend once taught her. Sarain then carried these supplies to where they were needed.

When she arrived Sarain just stared up at the X for a moment before preparing what she needed to do. A few vil sangs passed her curiously as they enter the club.

The door guard watched unsure of what to make of it, debating whether or not to get the owners. Sarain then approached the guard with a package in hand. He went to stop her from entering, but before he could, she quickly stabbed him in the chest with her machete. The large vil sang toppled over, and Sarain walked inside. She made her way through the building, placing down packages without a bother. The crowd simply watched as Sarain worked at scattering packages until one vil sang finally realized what she was doing.

"Those are bombs!" the vil sang shouted, and within seconds the crowd was rushing and screaming to get out. Sarain went about her business undisturbed, and then finally the owners appeared. The two demonic vil sangs approached Sarain, their eyes settled on and glaring at her.

"What do you think you are doing?" one of the beasts asked. "Closing your club," Sarain replied. The other creature then stepped forward and told her, "We may have been ordered not to kill you, but nothing was said about maiming."

Sarain withdrew her machete, and raised it into the air as she stated, "You can try." The first beast lunged at her with its fangs and claws ready. Sarain dodged his attack, and swung her machete into its back. She sliced deep into its back, but did not kill the creature. The second beast went for Sarain, she ducked as it flew over her, its claws grazing into her back, but her machete drove into its chest. It fell to the ground and no longer moved, and the first beast was angered by this. He came at Sarain again, and she swung at it once more. The large gargoyle-ish vil sang grabbed her machete by the blade in mid swing, its hand not hurt by it, and crushed the machete till half the blade broke off. The creature seemed pleased with itself, but Sarain was not fazed, she quickly plunged the rest of the machete into the creature's chest, and forced it in until her own hand was inside the beast and its heart was pierced.

The creature looked surprised just before it closed its eyes. Sarain let go of her machete, and the beast collapsed to the ground. Sarain looked at her hands to see that they had been covered with even more blood, and she felt her own trickling down her back. The owners out of the way should have brought Sarain some relief, but the night's events still weighed heavy on her.

Sarain continued setting up her explosives with no more interruptions. She rigged the explosives to blow with a switch just as Winston had taught her when they blew up the Purge. When she was done she stepped outside into the cool night air, she walked a distance away from the club to where Eddie used to pick her up after a long night of hunting. His face flashed into her mind as she flipped the switch. She almost didn't hear the explosion.

Sarain opened her eyes to a world of flames; the club laid in ruins as the rumble burned. The fire danced higher with each blow of the cold night breeze. She watched for a moment as the flames burned all that they could, and though they were nowhere near Sarain, she felt that they were burning away the last two years she had spent in the city; everything she had worked for was gone just as quickly as the X.

Sarain let the switch fall from her blood soaked hands; it hit the ground with a clatter. She finally turned to leave, but was stopped short when she saw a familiar face staring back at her.

"You weren't going to leave without saying goodbye?" James asked in a smug and phony tone.

Chapter 29

Sarain stared at James in silence; her once friend now seemed like a stranger. With his sandy blond hair and green eyes, he looked the same, but now appeared completely different. He was not her friend, but in fact her enemy; she knew this now, and his boyish charms no longer had an effect on her.

"You're quiet," James remarked, breaking the silence, "Have you nothing to say to me?" Sarain didn't answer right away, but when she did, she replied, "You were working for my father all along, weren't you?"

James smiled and answered, "I was doing as told." "You were the one that tipped him off when Desmina told me the truth about what I am?" she deciphered. "What can I say, I fake unconscious well," he said with a smirk.

"And your kids? Did they even have names?" Sarain asked him, her anger growing. "You know, I didn't ask them before killing them," James responded with a chuckle, "Maybe next time."

"Was anything you told me true?" Sarain asked blankly. "Does it really matter?" James replied. "No...

No it doesn't," she said softly. James took a step closer to Sarain, and said, "I've been doing this for a very long time, but I have to say, you have been my favorite assignment."

"Assignment," Sarain repeated, disgusted by the word. "Yes, your father wanted me to help you adjust to the changes you're going through, and he figured having you help us take out Desmina and Cyrus would be a good way for us to bond," he explained.

"You planned everything?" Sarain asked, but it came out as more of a statement. James then took another step closer to Sarain while saying, "Our meeting may have been staged, but I never planned on my feelings for you being real." He continued approaching Sarain, his hand went out to her, and he ran his fingers over her hair.

"Don't touch me," she muttered, but James didn't stop. He took a hold of her by the back of her neck and pulled her to him. He whispered, "You are worn and unarmed, even if you wanted to fight me, you wouldn't have the strength."

James pressed his lips against Sarain's, she didn't pull away, but she didn't return the kiss. James was right, she was tired, and her machete was gone. The night had been long and hard on Sarain, her body was beaten and sore, and the way she was now was hardly a match for even a regular vil sang.

James broke the kiss, and softly said to Sarain, "See, you're totally helpless to me." He then caressed her cheek and leaned into her ear, and whispered, "We'd be perfect together."

The words echoed in Sarain's head, and she wondered if this too had been arranged by her father; he hadn't wanted her with a mortal, and he had sent James to her before. "You don't love me," Sarain remarked. James kissed her neck passionately, and answered, "I want you just the same."

"Eddie loved me," she muttered. James stopped kissing her for a moment, and was silent before finally responding, "You should have chosen me." Sarain was motionless after James spoke, his words put a tinge in her heart, and she listened intently as he said, "I was supposed to lure you away from that mortal, and when you didn't come to me, that's when your father decided to take more drastic measures."

"He had planned to kill him all along?" Sarain weakly asked. "If he hadn't I would have, whatever it would take to bring you to me," James whispered back. Sarain felt the anger growing inside her; neither James nor her father cared about her feelings, they just wanted her as a prize, as a pawn in some game of theirs. Eddie had been the only one looking out for her wellbeing, and Sarain had fought him for so long that it got him killed.

"I'm not going with you," Sarain muttered to James. He ran his fingers through her hair and simply stated, "Yes you are; you need me to help you through the changes you are going through." "I don't want your help," she said to him, frustrated by his persistence. James then took a hold of a handful of Sarain's hair and gave it a tug, and said, "You have no idea how to deal with what you are going through, and what's to come. You can't do it on your own!"

Sarain then pulled back from James, and he saw that her eyes were glowing, and with this he commented, "That is only the beginning." Then Sarain's eyes started to flare up even more and she opened her mouth to speak, exposing her fangs, "I think I'll manage."

James stared her in the face with a smug expression on his as he stated, "You're not ready to be a monster." Sarain looked into his eyes, and said with all honesty, "Being a monster is the easy part." Suddenly Sarain lunged towards James, and knocked him to the ground. She pinned him down, and before he could react, she sank her teeth into his throat. James let out a painful cry as he tried to pull Sarain off of him, but she only clenched down harder.

James' blood rushed into Sarain's mouth and down her throat. It felt cold as it dribbled down her chin, and it tasted bitter and old. He continued to struggle as Sarain bit down again, a gurgling sound rising from his throat. She chewed at him, swallowing his flesh with each breath she took, until James no longer fought. When Sarain finally pried herself away from him, he laid still in a pool of his own blood, nearly decapitated; James was dead.

Sarain was once again covered in fresh blood, but this time she simply reacted by wiping her mouth. Now was the time for her to be the monster.

Sarain got home just before dawn. She showered and packed before the sun had a chance to rise. She took one bag filled with a few items of clothes, the hunter's journal, and her backup machete. She wore her ankh around her neck, and held a few items in her hands.

Sarain couldn't bear to look at anything in her home, everything reminded her of Eddie. She was once again going to have to start anew; another city, another life. Sarain stood in front of her house as she watched flames engulf her once home, and she knew that if there wasn't a place to come back to then she would never return. The fire danced with intense fury, and Sarain was a silent spectator.

She looked down at the items she held; two pictures and a ring. She took a hold of the ring first and thought of Eddie, he had wanted her to be his wife, but Sarain knew that she in that role was just as unlikely as it was of her ever seeing Eddie again. She looked at the ring one last time and then threw it into the fire. Next she held her mother's picture, the only one she had. Ariana held her dearly, and no matter what her grandfather may have told her, Sarain knew her mother had loved her. But the picture had been tarnished by the scribbled words of Aion telling her to meet her at the molasses factory, and the photograph now reminded her of her failure and loss of Eddie. She threw it too into the fire.

Lastly, Sarain held the photograph of her and Orran; two friends, both secretly crushing for each other. She recalled the argument she had had with Eddie when he discovered his resemblance to Orran, and his accusation of her using him as a replacement. She went to toss the picture into the fire, and the sudden flash of Orran's face leaning in to kiss her made Sarain stop. The picture was too dear to her to part with, and she placed it into her bag.

And suddenly Sarain felt guilty, while she should be grieving Eddie, she suddenly found herself grieving Orran, and realized that losing Eddie was like losing her old friend all over again. Sarain stood there in amazement as the revelation came to her that she was still in love with Orran, and that she had always been.

Had Eddie been right all along? The idea of it made Sarain quiver, and she thought, "Oh god, I am a monster."

End of Book 2

Continue Sarain's adventure in Vile Blood 3: Reunion available in ebook and soon to be in print!

Thanks for reading!

Jen Golembiewski